Dedicated to all the pilgrims, past, present and future
May God bless you on your journeys with insight, love, and mercy.

The whole journey of life is a journey of preparation…to see, to feel, to understand the beauty of what lies ahead, of the homeland towards which we walk.

—Pope Francis, April 2013

CONTENTS

INTRODUCTION

People have been telling stories since the dawn of the human race. Jesus was famous for it; he told many stories in the form of parables. It was the main way he taught the crowds who flocked to see him.

This tradition of using storytelling to pass on important truths was a part of the Church for a long time. From Dante Alighieri to all those medieval legends and on to Thomas More, Catholic storytelling has added to the richness of human wisdom and of the human experience.

That's why it was odd that it appeared to die away for a few hundred years. Perhaps it was the Enlightenment with its penchant for skepticism, but the example that Jesus set seemed to have been set aside for a time by many Catholic writers.

Happily, the telling of stories picked up in the modern era. Writers like J.R.R. Tolkien, G.K. Chesterton, Flannery O'Connor, and Evelyn Waugh have all enriched our lives, even though the genres their works appeared in varied enormously. From fantasy to detective stories to contemporary fiction and even what is generically called "dark" fiction, modern Catholic writers have enriched not only Catholic culture but the world's culture.

It's been said that the Golden Age of Catholic Fiction died out a couple of generations ago, but that isn't true; there are many contemporary authors who carry on the tradition of the great literary giants of the past. Do you want Anglo-Saxon heroines? Nosy church ladies who solve mysteries? Nuns in space? Time-traveling bunnies? Everyday people trying to find love? All these characters are alive and well and living in the pages of contemporary Catholic fiction.

You'll find samples of some of this variety here in this anthology. The authors are as different from one another as the genres they represent, but they all have one thing in common: They are all members of the Catholic Writers Guild.

The Guild was formed in 2007 as an online forum whose members helped one another with the writing and marketing of their books. It quickly developed into an international community dedicated to the rebirth of Catholic writing. Their only requirement for membership is that "members be faithful to Catholic teaching and that their writing reflects that." This holds true for both fiction and nonfiction.

This is the Guild's first published anthology, and for our "first ever," we chose short fiction under the theme of Pilgrimage. Our purpose is to showcase the skills of the authors involved, as well as to introduce readers to genres that they perhaps did not realize were represented in Catholic fiction.

In this collection you will find historical fiction, sci-fi/fantasy, romance; there is even a ghost story. Whatever the genre, each story endeavors in its own way to further the increase of beauty in the world while remaining faithful to the teachings of the Magisterium.

It is our sincerest hope that this anthology accomplishes that.

Enjoy—and if you do, we encourage you to do a little digging on your own and look for more. Catholic storytelling is alive and well. It's just looking for readers like you.

A PILGRIM'S ROMANCE

Nancy Bechel

Four in the morning was a ludicrous hour to be awake. Especially voluntarily. Under normal circumstances, nothing would have possessed me to drag my groggy self out of my dorm room this early, let alone drive off into the darkness with a collection of my best friends. I loved them, but friendship had its limits. Those limits started a good hour after sun-up.

There was only one person who could motivate me to do something so ridiculous as to set off for a hike through the mountains before dawn: Jeremy.

We pulled to a stop in the meager parking lot at the base of the trailhead as first light turned everything gray. My roommate, Celia, leaped from the back seat with all the annoying vigor of a morning person who'd already had three cups of coffee.

"C'mon, Bernadette!" she cried, yanking me after her with a pull on my elbow. As I stumbled from the car, she put her hands on her hips and took a deep breath in through her nose. "Just smell that fresh air! It's better than caffeine."

"I'd rather have caffeine," I grumbled.

"I brought a carafe with me, if you didn't get your morning cup."

I spun toward the sound of the warm, masculine voice. Only a few feet behind me, Jeremy stood with a metal thermos in one hand and a smile spread across his amused face. He wasn't traditionally handsome, per se, but one look at that smile and his sparkling eyes was all the jolt I needed.

"Oh, uh, sure. Why not?" I quickly smoothed my hair and my rumpled clothes, hoping that I didn't have drool on my chin from my nap on the way here.

Jeremy turned toward the rest of our group, who were also climbing out of their cars in various states of dishevelment. "Anyone else for coffee?" A chorus of assent sounded around the parking lot. Jeremy glanced back at me with a wink. "Sounds like you're not the only one who prefers caffeine."

I felt a blush rise to my cheeks. "Oh, it's not that I don't like fresh air..." I started to protest, but he had already returned to his car to retrieve two more carafes. I sighed.

"Smooth, Bernadette," Celia teased under her breath.

I groaned. I'd been hoping to impress him with my enthusiasm for the outdoors, since this whole hiking pilgrimage with Fr. Brennan was Jeremy's idea to begin with. But it seemed I was going to continue to be less than his ideal girl, no matter how hard I tried.

Celia put an arm around my shoulders and gave me a little squeeze. "Don't worry, BD, he likes you. It's obvious to all of us."

I gave her a skeptical look, but it was nice to have some reassurance that I wasn't just imagining things. After three years at college together, hanging out with the same friends, sharing so many interests, studying and working and praying alongside one another, I was nearly certain that Jeremy liked me as much as I liked him. But he'd never acted on it. It was starting to make me wonder if the chemistry between us was all in my head.

Celia gave me another squeeze of encouragement before we went arm in arm to receive our morning pick-me-up.

After a prayer and a blessing, we all donned our packs and followed Fr. Brennan onto the trailhead. Now that we were all filled with caffeine and the sky grew pink and gold with morning light, our group of fifteen was chatty and eager for the days ahead. Jeremy flitted around from group to group all morning, checking that everyone was okay and had what they needed. It was endearing to watch. He was so good at taking care of people. It was one of the reasons I liked him so much.

The third time Jeremy checked in with Celia and me, he lingered. The three of us chatted like we always do, so familiar, so easy, so...homey. I could chat with Jeremy for the rest of my life and never tire of it. *Please, God?*

"So, Jeremy..." The tone in Celia's voice immediately put me on guard, and I glanced at her warily. "You know how you named this 'The JPII Pilgrimage' because of all the mountain hikes JPII took young people on while he was a priest in Poland?"

"Yeah. What about it?" Jeremy didn't seem to notice that Celia was setting him up, but I gave her a warning glare. She grinned at me.

"Well, there were a lot of marriages that came out of those hikes."

I elbowed her.

"Oof!" Celia rubbed her side, but didn't stop. "Apparently, not one of those couples got a divorce. Pretty good odds, huh?"

I chanced a sidelong look at Jeremy. He seemed unfazed. Either he hadn't picked up on her not-so-subtle hints, or he was ignoring them.

"John Paul II was amazing," Jeremy affirmed with an appreciative nod. "He's one of my heroes."

Celia hooked a thumb at me. "Bernadette loves JPII, too."

I nearly glared at her again, but a millisecond later, I was glad I didn't. I would have missed the way Jeremy smiled at me.

"I know," he said. I nearly melted.

Celia glanced behind us, then up ahead again. "So, I have some theories," she said, lowering her voice as she leaned toward us conspiratorially. "Who out of our group is going to end up together, do you think?"

I could have strangled her.

Jeremy's cheeks flushed, and his ears turned bright pink. He cleared his throat, which I knew meant he was nervous. "Oh...I...think that's above my pay grade." He laughed it off, but I could tell the question had made him uncomfortable.

"Oh, come on," Celia pressed, "you have to have some guesses! I mean, Isaac and Maddie, for instance. They've already started talking about getting engaged. Rachel and Vianney have been together for a year. And even though Emma and Joe have only been on a few dates, I won't be surprised at all if they end up together." She looked pointedly at me. "And there are a few others who might be dating by the end of the pilgrimage, don't you think?"

My face was probably three shades of crimson, and I could no longer muster the gumption to look at Jeremy.

He cleared his throat again. Then a third time. Ugh, this was torture!

"Uh, Jeremy," I interjected, "I don't remember, when did Fr. Brennan say we were stopping for lunch?"

Jeremy glanced down at his watch. "Shouldn't be too much longer." He sounded like he was hoping it would be immediately, like I was.

I pointed a casual finger toward the front of the group where Father was leading the pack. "Could I ask you to check with him, to find out how far we are from our picnic spot?"

Jeremy immediately perked up. "Sure thing!" And without any further encouragement, he shot ahead of us on the trail.

"Argh, BD!" Celia whined. "We had him right where we wanted him! Why did you have to give him an easy out?"

I scowled at her. "That is not where I want him, Cel. Couldn't you see how embarrassed he was? Why did you do that?" I couldn't keep the anger from my voice.

"Tsk. My dear roomie, some men are extremely slow movers. Sometimes they need an extra push to step up and be men."

"Not like that," I snipped.

Celia shook her head at me. "I don't know what you're so mad about. It's not like I said anything about you and him, specifically. If that's what he read into my words, that's on him."

I rolled my eyes. "Oh yes, you were sooo subtle."

She sniffed. "I was subtle, thank you. Just wait, when he asks you out sometime this weekend, he'll say that this conversation was what finally convinced him to man up."

"Right."

She nudged me with her elbow. "Have a little confidence, BD. You're amazing. He'll come to his senses, just you wait and see."

I was still annoyed, but I couldn't help but hope she was right.

Our picnic spot was worth the morning climb. A small clearing opened up to a view down into the valley we'd climbed out of, with gentle peaks on either side gradually rising to more strenuous heights.

Fr. Brennan gathered us all in a circle, blessed our meals, and invited us to sit.

"Have all of you considered what you're seeking on pilgrimage?" he asked as we began to chomp on our well-earned lunches. He was met with various states of confirmation and indecision. "Anyone care to share?"

A nervous twinge pricked me. I didn't dare share what I really wanted from this pilgrimage. But one by one, everyone in the group began to speak up. I couldn't be the only one to remain silent.

When it seemed I could avoid it no longer, I swallowed hard. "I just want the grace and courage to say yes to God's will, whatever that might be." It wasn't really a lie. I did want to say yes to God's will. I just had a very particular vision of what God's will ought to be.

Without meaning to, I glanced at Jeremy. He was watching me with a strange expression on his face, almost as if what I'd said caused him pain. It made me nervous. He had yet to share what he was hoping to get from this pilgrimage, even though he was the one who wanted to do the hike in the first place. Our eyes met for the briefest moment, but as the next person began to speak, he looked away. Not for the first time, I wished I could read his mind.

Every person shared, until all that was left was Jeremy and Fr. Brennan. I held my breath as Jeremy gripped his knees and stared at the ground in front of himself. He cleared his throat, and took a sideways glance at Father. Father nodded slightly. I looked back and forth between them. What was going on? The thought flitted through my head that maybe Jeremy was about to ask me out, right here, in front of all of our friends, with Father's approval. My stomach began to flutter, and I bit my lip in anticipation.

"So... I've only mentioned this to Fr. Brennan until now, but..." Jeremy rocked back slightly where he sat, and looked up again. Right at me. "I've actually been accepted to seminary. I'll be going there in the fall instead of finishing my degree at Sheene U."

Everything stopped. My heart. My breath. The whole world on its axis.

An empty pit opened up in the middle of my chest, and all I could feel was pain.

Wide eyes all around the clearing looked back and forth between Jeremy and myself. Apparently, Celia wasn't the only one who'd had theories about who would end up together. I wanted to run. To hide. To sob until I had no tears left. But I didn't want to make a scene. I forced a smile that I was sure everyone knew was fake, and wrestled out a feeble, "Congratulations."

This started a cascade of similar remarks from around the circle, but I could barely hear them. Beside me, Celia gripped my arm in a show of support, but I couldn't look at her. If I did, I knew I would cry.

"Thanks, guys." Jeremy's voice shook a little. It was tearing me apart. I stared at the ground in cold shock. "I didn't want to say anything until I knew for sure. I mean, if I wasn't accepted, I didn't want it to be a big deal. But now... I guess I'm looking for the grace and courage to say yes to God's will, too."

No. He didn't get to say that. He didn't get to use my words against me that way. This wasn't what I had meant. I didn't want this. And I couldn't take it anymore.

I stood on impulse, leaving my pack, my lunch, everything, lying there in the grass, and took off down the trail we'd just climbed.

"Let her go, Jeremy," Fr. Brennan said behind me. Thank God. I didn't want to talk to him.

Besides, I'd be safe. I had felt Celia get up when I did, and knew she wouldn't leave me alone, even if I wanted her to.

I marched downhill until the reality of what Jeremy had just said sank in, and the strength went out of my legs. I sank to the ground in the middle of the path, and finally let the tears come.

A few moments later, warm arms wrapped around me. Celia's voice said, "Oh honey, I'm so sorry," as she petted my hair and let me cry.

As my tears soaked my sleeves, I berated myself. What had I been thinking? Why was I even upset? Jeremy had never been anything but friendly toward me. He'd never given me any indication that he intended to ask me out. He was sweet towards me, but he was sweet towards everyone. Sometimes I thought he was flirting, but maybe he didn't realize I was taking it that way. We were close, sure, but that wasn't exactly a marriage proposal. I'd built all of my hopes and dreams on assumptions.

Jeremy was going to be a priest.

Maybe he'll discern out after a year or two?

The thought quieted my tears at last. Yes, maybe this was only temporary. Maybe this was one of those things where God had a bigger plan, and He would return Jeremy to me after a little while.

But even as I thought it, a nagging sense tickled the back of my mind, like that wasn't the proper attitude at all.

Still, it was the only hope I could hold onto at the moment. So hold on, I did.

When Celia and I finally returned to the group, they were playing Frisbee like nothing had happened. I avoided looking at Jeremy, and he didn't try to talk to me. Everyone else just pretended they hadn't seen anything.

As we set off again, Fr. Brennan beckoned me up to the front of the group with him. I obeyed self-consciously, aware that everyone behind us could see me.

"How are you doing?" Father asked with his characteristic kindness.

That's the kind of priest Jeremy would be, too.

The thought leaped to my mind unbidden, and I pushed it away.

I shrugged in response.

"Jeremy's news came as quite a shock, I imagine."

I swallowed. "Yeah."

"Do you want to talk about it?"

I didn't answer right away. "I feel like an idiot."

Father gave me a compassionate smile. "You don't have anything to be ashamed of."

My throat tightened with emotion. "I completely misread everything," I choked out. "All this time he was just being nice, and I thought... I thought..." I couldn't finish, but sniffed and wiped the back of my hand across my eyes.

Father was quiet until I regained control. "I can't speak for Jeremy, Bernadette, but it is not my impression that you were misreading how things are. Though I'm not sure how much of a comfort that is to you."

Wait, what? Father thought Jeremy liked me, too?

"I don't know if this will comfort you at all either, but," Fr. Brennan glanced back at the group behind us, then faced forward again, "I was engaged to be married before I finally made the decision to break it off and follow the call God placed on my heart for the priesthood."

I stared at him. "You were?"

He nodded. "High school sweethearts. I proposed our junior year in college, and we were planning to marry after graduation."

"What happened?" I wasn't sure I wanted to know.

"I went on silent retreat over spring break senior year. When I finally slowed down enough to let God get a word in edgewise, I realized I'd been running from a desire God had placed on my heart since childhood. Because I wanted what I wanted." Father gave me a knowing smile. "Breaking up with my fiancée was the most difficult decision I've ever made. It was incredibly painful for both of us, but I've never regretted it."

"Where is she now?" I asked, out of morbid curiosity.

"Married to an amazing Catholic man. They have eight kids, a hobby farm, and her oldest just joined a convent right out of high school."

I stared at the rocky path in front of me. Whatever point Father was trying to make, I didn't want to hear it. "Okay, well, thanks for the pep talk. I think I'm going to go find Celia."

"Bernadette." The tone in Father's voice stopped me before I ran away. "Sometimes what feels like the end is just the start of something better."

My chest clenched like my heart was foam in a vice, but I nodded in polite acknowledgement before running off to find Celia.

When the sun hung low in the sky, we finally reached the summit. Father started doling out tasks to ready us for our night on the mountaintop, and when he asked for a volunteer to collect firewood, I leaped at it. Anything to get me away from the surreptitious glances of pity from my friends. But I nearly recanted when Jeremy raised his hand.

"I'll go, too."

"Great," said Fr. Brennan. "Bernadette and Jeremy, go collect firewood. Be quick about it—you don't want to miss the sunset!"

Celia leaned over and whispered, "Do you want me to swap with you?"

I glanced at Jeremy as he made his way toward me. He'd avoided me all afternoon, as I'd avoided him. Maybe now was as good a time as any to talk.

I shook my head. "Thanks anyway."

She squeezed my arm. "You've got this, BD."

I nodded with more confidence than I felt. Celia glared at Jeremy as he joined us, and he had the decency to look sheepish.

"Ready?" he asked.

I nearly said "no," but nodded instead.

We went off a little way down the path, out of earshot and eyesight of the rest of the group. If Jeremy hadn't just announced to everyone that anything romantic between us was impossible, there would probably have been some teasing questions about what we'd been up to when we got back. But as it was, no one was likely to say anything now.

It was a silly thing to be bitter about, but I was.

Neither Jeremy nor I said anything as we began to pick up various pieces of downed wood near the edge of the path. As the silence wore on and our pile grew, I began to wonder if maybe he wasn't going to say anything at all. The tension between us was unfamiliar, and more than a little uncomfortable. Nothing like how things had been only hours ago.

I could feel him looking at me, and I finally stopped and turned to face him. He stood on the opposite side of the path, our pile of fire-wood between us, just watching.

"What?" I asked, irritation all too obvious in my voice.

He fidgeted with a branch. "I... I'm sorry."

"For what?"

He glanced down, turning the branch over in his hands. "I should have told you. Before today. I see that now."

I turned away, swallowing the tightness in my throat, and blinking back the tears that stung my eyes. "None of my business," I choked out.

"I don't know. It kind of was. I mean…" He took a deep breath and sighed. "I was kind of leading you on."

I glanced at him sharply.

"I know this isn't an excuse, but it's been really hard, discerning the priesthood." He bent the branch, curling it back on itself. It was clearly too green to be firewood. Why had he even bothered to pick it up? "I've known for a long time that God was asking me to consider it, but… In all honesty, I wasn't ready to give up on, you know…everything else."

Jeremy looked up at me, a pleading look in his eyes. He wanted me to understand. I wasn't feeling particularly understanding.

"I don't know, actually," I said, tossing my own branch onto the pile.

Jeremy swallowed, and turned the branch over again. "I've wanted to ask you out for a long time," he said quietly. "I actually really like you, Bernadette."

My breath caught. My heart thrummed in my ears. I was finally hearing the words I'd longed to hear from him since I first got to know him freshman year, but they were colored with bitter disappointment.

"But, um…" Fidget. Fidget. "Every time I was about to ask you, it was like my guardian angel put his hand right here." Jeremy pressed a hand to the middle of his chest. "And I knew it wouldn't be fair. It wouldn't be fair to you. Because I already knew where God was calling me. And asking you out would just prolong…all of it. It would be selfish of me, ya know? Because I knew it would only be temporary. And I didn't want…"

He faltered, playing with the branch again. "JPII always talked about how real love means taking responsibility for the other person, looking out for their good, even when it's not what you want." Jeremy coiled the branch and uncoiled it again. "If I asked you out just because I wanted to be with you, even though I knew I'd have to break it off, that wouldn't be love, ya know?"

Fresh tears blurred my eyes. The ache in my chest opened up again, but what had been emptiness was now a flood of affection, admiration, and bitter longing.

He was so good. Why was he so good? I was tempted to curse him for his virtue, his consideration of me, his selfless choice to deny what he wanted for my sake. Part of me wanted to argue that it would have been worth it, just to belong to him for a little while. But even as I thought it, I realized that it wouldn't have been true. I wouldn't have belonged to him. Not really. Because I wasn't his. Just as he wasn't really mine. Jeremy was a gift, but he was a gift that wasn't meant for me. He was meant for the Church. The world. For Christ. And that wouldn't change, no matter how tightly I held onto him.

Open your hands, Beloved.

The words flitted through my heart as I fought the tears that blurred my eyes.

I don't want to, I replied, every part of me aching.

Open your hands, Beloved.

I turned around and covered my face. *How could You be so cruel? Jeremy cares about me, and I care about him. Why shouldn't we be together?*

Open your hands, Beloved.

I don't want to! I repeated. Everything in me ached. I'd held onto the hope of being with Jeremy for so many years. How was I just supposed to let go? Just like that? *Why, Lord? Why do I have to let go?*

Then the words came to me, like the gentle balm of a breeze on a hot day.

How else can I give you everything I have in store?

Something released inside me, and the flood gates opened. I tried to hold back the tears, but it was no use. A gentle hand touched my shoulder, and I turned without thinking. I buried myself in Jeremy's chest, and for a moment, I thought he would push me away. But then his arms wrapped around me, and I could no longer hold back my sobs. I was being selfish, but I couldn't pretend to be as good as Jeremy.

"I'm sorry, Bernadette. I'm so sorry…"

He repeated his apology over and over as he held me. My tears of sadness mingled with anger, but not at Jeremy. If God was calling him to the priesthood, how could he say anything but yes? No, if I was honest, it wasn't Jeremy I was angry with at all. I was angry with God. For asking me to give him up. For putting this amazing man in front of me, and then telling me he was off limits. For giving me so much hope, and then dashing it all to pieces.

Do you think he is the only wonderful man I've made, Beloved? The question hovered in the space between my sobs, almost amused, and ever so loving. It nearly made me even more angry, that the Lord could be amused when I was in so much pain, but there was so much compassion in the question, I couldn't ignore it.

Do you think I cannot bring another such man into your life?

I knew the "right" answer was no, that I didn't have those doubts, but as I shook in Jeremy's arms, I realized the truth. In my mind, and in my heart, Jeremy had been the only one. For years. To the point where I had come on this pilgrimage for him, and not for God.

A homily Fr. Brennan had given only a few weeks ago flitted through my mind. "Who is first in your heart?" he had asked. At the time, I thought I knew the answer. But the truth struck me with a deep conviction, and I was suddenly ashamed.

It sobered me.

Gradually, my tears lessened. I drew back from Jeremy, wiping my eyes on my sleeves. He released me and took a step back.

"Here."

I glanced up. He was holding out an old-fashioned handkerchief. The fact that he used them was one of the odd quirks that had endeared him to me. I accepted with a watery smile.

"Sorry," I said as I blew my nose. "I didn't mean to go to pieces on you."

"I didn't mean to hurt you."

His quiet admission only deepened my awareness of how kind he was. My heart gave a fond ache.

"You didn't do anything wrong," I said at last, then laughed a little. "Well, maybe you could have told me all this in private before the big announcement, so it wasn't such a shock, but other than that..." I smiled sadly. "You never gave me any indication that you intended for us to be more than friends. I just...hoped."

I held his handkerchief out, and he took it, gazing down at it as he turned it in his hands.

"I hoped, too," he admitted.

Was his heart also breaking? The thought lit a fire in me, but one that surprised even myself.

"You'll be an amazing priest, Jeremy, if that's what God is calling you to."

His eyes leaped to my face. "Really?" The self-doubt I saw in them rent my heart. Didn't he know how amazing he was?

I swallowed once, and summoned my courage. "Really. The way you take care of everyone. You're so good at recognizing the needs of people around you, and being there for them when they need it. You have a big heart. You're super generous with your time and talents. You'll be a good father to any parish God gives you."

Now that I said it aloud, I realized how true it was. Father Jeremy would be beloved everywhere he went.

I mustered a genuine smile. "I can't wait to see what amazing things God does with you."

Jeremy's eyes filled with moisture for the first time, and he clenched his teeth, one muscle twitching in his jaw. When he found words at last, he said, "Thanks, Bernadette. That means a lot. Coming from you."

"Well, I mean it." And I was surprised to find that I did.

He nodded and brushed at his cheek with the heel of one hand. "Hey, we should get this firewood back to camp. It's getting dark."

We gathered up our pile and walked together in silence. We arrived in time to see the last beautiful moments of sunset, and no one asked what took us so long.

When Celia asked me what happened before bed, I wasn't ready to talk about it, and she—mercifully—let it go.

Fr. Brennan woke us all for Mass at dawn. He raised the Eucharist as the first light of day broke over the horizon, flooding us all with a golden glow. For the first time since I'd heard Jeremy's news the day before, I felt a sense of peace and well-being, like everything was going to be okay.

In that moment, I had a vision. It was Jeremy standing in Fr. Brennan's place, robed in priestly vestments and glowing in the light of a golden morning. All around him were gathered countless people of every age and background, the fruits of his labors, souls won for Christ because of his sacrifice. The beauty of it took my breath away. And when I cried, they were tears of joy.

See what I can do when you let go, Beloved?

The gentle question brought a bitter-sweet smile to my lips.

Yes, Lord, I see.

Once more, the invitation came. *Open your hands, Beloved.*

As I returned from receiving Communion and knelt in the grass on the summit, I laid my hands in my lap, palms up, and slowly opened them. It felt strange. Frightening, even. But also freeing. And as I let go of the dreams and plans I'd pursued for the past three years, I offered the most genuine prayer I'd prayed in a long time.

Whatever Your will, whatever that means, I give You permission, Lord.

I opened my eyes to see Jeremy kneeling in prayer by the make-shift altar.

Thy will be done.

And I meant it.

SURRENDER

Isabelle Wood

So, I'll be first to die.

Well, not first, technically speaking. Steven had already been stoned. But first of the twelve. James certainly hadn't expected that.

And yet—the guards gave him a rough shove, sending him stumbling through the palace gate into the dusty street packed tight with jeering crowds—what he'd expected even less was the awed wonder that this honor would fall to him. Like any sane person would call death an honor. But being found worthy to die for Jesus…

James found an absurd smile tickling his mouth even as his heart pounded and his palms sweated with the natural human fear of dying. Was this what Steven had felt like?

"Move! All of you, out of the way!" Slowed nearly to a halt by the pressing crowds, two of King Herod's guards kept hold of James' arms while the other two forced people aside with their spear shafts.

James stumbled, his knee hitting a cobblestone with a jolt before the guards jerked him back to his feet. He limped now, knee throbbing, and his hands, on the other side of his bound wrists behind his back, tingled and stung.

Not like any of that mattered when he was minutes from being beheaded with the sword.

As the guards continued to jostle him along, James scanned the faces in the crowd, hoping they'd read the peace in his face, hoping they'd find the same hope he had. Strangers, all of them. Looking away, most of them.

Then one young man caught his eye, held his gaze, and the breath left James' lungs.

John.

What was his brother doing here? He was going to get himself caught and killed.

John's eyes were red, and he alone stood silent, jostled along in the surging crowd but without seeming to notice, gaze steady and fixed on James.

It seemed an age, but a moment later, John was swept away from James' sight, leaving James with a sudden pit of unease in his stomach. Not just unease his younger brother would be caught, but an unease that ran deeper, suddenly threatening to snatch away his peace.

This was it.

After today—the next quarter hour, even—he'd do no more preaching, no more teaching, no more spreading the gospel to the ends of the earth. He'd never even made it to the ends of the earth, never made any holy journeys beyond the confines of Israel. He'd die here, instead. In Judea, a forgotten little corner of the Roman Empire where he'd spent his entire life.

It wasn't quite that he didn't trust Peter, John, and the others to take the gospel there eventually, but...he'd no longer be a part of it. His pilgrimage in this life was over. His mission, ended. He'd no longer have a say, no longer be present to help and protect the others. And without his protection—without his role—could the followers of Jesus even survive?

Would the good news of Jesus, would John, would any of it even make it outside Israel, or would everyone and everything be lost to time? Despair reared, threatening.

No longer paying the road any attention, James stumbled, missing the shift uphill, and sent himself and a guard careening into the pressing crowd for a moment. His surroundings crashed back over him.

The cursing guards, the screaming crowds, the jeering and jostling, even the looming, tight-packed mudbrick buildings and street stalls, all added to the claustrophobia and commotion James felt. The sweat and excrement of the streets stung his nose, and dust clung to his sweaty skin and filthy tunic. The sun beating down on his head only added to his discomfort. His knee still throbbed.

James watched his bare feet shuffle along as the road continued its ascent, fading to dust instead of the cobbled stones that surrounded Herod's palace. He hoped the crowd couldn't read his face now. The uncertainty, the unease, the...distrust. Shame heated his face, but it was true.

He didn't trust that this could work without him.

From the time he was a boy, almost too young to even walk, he'd insisted on accompanying his abba on their fishing boat, somehow not able to grasp that Zebedee could catch any fish without his help. He would accompany his younger brother everywhere, even on errands Abba had sent John alone on, just to make sure John did what he was supposed to...and without getting hurt. And now, he found his familiar prayer to God rising to his thoughts: *Adonai, give me control.*

But things weren't in his control anymore.

And—with a lurch of his stomach—James realized that scared him more than even the fact he'd die in minutes.

He swallowed and glanced up, catching sight of the looming walls and open gates ahead to the garrison where his execution would take place. A sheen of cold sweat shivered across his suddenly clammy skin, and he found his breaths and heartbeat coming faster.

No, he couldn't die. Not yet, honor or no. He still had too much left to do. The others needed him still. John—

James suddenly caught sight of his brother again, shoving back into the crowd from some side street and craning until his eyes found James', and a jolt shot through James.

For some reason, when John's gaze locked on his, a flash of memory turned it into Jesus' gaze—piercing, penetrating, deep, convicting, and in this particular instance…rebuking.

The memory flashed back to him suddenly, clear as a trumpet call. When a Samaritan village had refused to welcome Jesus, James—trying, again, to take control—had joined with John in asking if Jesus wanted them to send down fire from heaven. And Jesus…

Tears stung James' eyes, and he didn't bother blinking them away as they escaped down his cheeks into his beard.

Jesus had rebuked them, one line of his words piercing James' heart like a lance and imprinting itself in his mind. *Leave to God what is God's.* In that case, justice. In this case…

James sucked in a breath, opening eyes he hadn't realized he'd shut, realizing he'd lost sight of John again. But he could finally see himself. He needed to let go. He'd learned that before, of course, had let go again and again on his pilgrimage of following Jesus…of his job, his family, his possessions. His life, even. But on this final stage of his journey…

One thing, he still held on to.

Peace came back into sight, waiting, offering him the joy, resolve, and hope of a few minutes ago. But in return, it asked for only— James huffed wryly—well, everything.

His twitching mouth drew down again, and he looked up as they passed beneath the shadow of the gateway into the garrison, the crowd pressing in behind. He knew what he needed to do—knew he had precious little time left to do it—and yet, he hesitated. Simple, yes. Easy? No. But…worth it?

James exhaled, keenly aware of the cool stones of the paved court-yard with every step. Every step drawing closer to his last…closer to the execution block. Three...his heart fluttered. Two...his stomach lurched. One...he let out a breath and let go.

Your mission is Yours, Lord. A smile tickled his mouth again as the guards shoved him to his knees with a jolt, never to rise again. Peace returned. Jesus wouldn't abandon His Church and His followers...like he'd never abandoned James.

My pilgrimage is almost done.

The guards shoved James' torso down, pressing his neck into the wooden, splintered slot carved out for it, then slammed the top beam down, locking him in place. Ironic, really, since James had never felt so free.

As he waited for the blow of the sword, the jeers of the crowd...the shouts of the guards...the dust, smells, and sweat—all of it faded into the background.

A cool breeze tickled his face and ruffled his hair, and he pulled his gaze up to see that—above and beyond the rising towers of the garrison—storm clouds had begun to roll in. Thunder rumbled, reverberating deep in James' chest like a caress from the Father's hand.

Then, as the executioner stepped into place, tugging on his gloves in preparation to unsheathe his sword, John burst to the front of the crowd. He stopped shy of the open area around the execution block the guards were holding, but his eyes met James' for a final time. Doubt...dread...fear...grief...they all played in John's face.

But now, James felt only peace, joy...and hope. He smiled for his brother, praying with a final inhale that Adonai would send comfort and strength to John, Peter, all the brothers and sisters in the trials to come. And then he let it all go as the executioner drew and raised his gleaming blade.

I surrender, Jesus. I answer your call to come home.

Then the sword came down.

GOLD IN THEM HILLS

Karen Meyer

It's a bright Sunday morning and my phone jolts me out of a good dream. It's only 8:30, but it's my mother already, calling to ask if I'd like to come to church with her. Again. I say, "No, thanks," again, as civilly as possible, but that civility is wearing thinner than my ratty old pajamas.

"What are you up to today?" She tries to cover her sorrow with some polite conversation.

"Going for a hike in the Adirondacks." I don't mention that I'm still flat on my back staring up at the cobwebs in my bedroom, and that I probably would have stayed there until 11:45 if she hadn't called. Sunday is the new Saturday, and it's my own business how I spend it. If some residue of guilt is still keeping me from having a blast, at least I can say that it's a relief to do anything other than slumping in a wooden pew for fifty-five minutes. "I should get on the road before it gets too late."

She doesn't take the hint. "Have you got a map of the mountain?"

"Trails are clearly marked," I say tersely. "There'll be lots of other people there."

"Okay, that's good," she answers mildly. There is a long pause. "Any leads on a new job?"

"Not yet." Not surprising when I have all but given up on looking.

"Millie was talking to me the other day—"

"And what's she got to say?" I break in, hackles raised.

"She's sad because she feels like she didn't set a good example for you while you two were growing up. She wishes she'd made more time to listen to you."

Shame and irritation turn quickly to sarcasm. "Well, you can put her troubled mind to rest. I take full credit for all my terrible choices. I really should get on the road. I'll call you later this week."

I hang up and head to the kitchen to make some coffee. No clean cups. Along with church-going and job hunting, I have also recently ditched housecleaning. There are always some bumps in the road when rearranging priorities.

I'm up now, so I might as well actually go for that hike. I've got a new set of spikes for my old boots in case the trail is icy. I hope it won't be too muddy, although I expect there's still a fair bit of snow in the shady places. It's a last-minute plan, but it's a short hike—less than six miles, round trip—and it's not going to take me all day to walk up a big hill and back down again.

I make the two-hour drive to the trailhead, and I don't see anyone else starting out at the same time I am. Some hikers are coming off the trail just as I'm parking. I feel a touch of uneasiness about the time, but it's mid-April, and the days are growing longer. I'm sure there's not going to be any problem getting back to my car before nightfall. I think about my mom again, and her asking about a map. Like I'm too dumb to follow the trail markers, right? She didn't say that, of course, but it's so annoying to be spoken to like a child. I've had enough of other people's direction. I spend the hike up muttering all the things I want to say to my mom, but can't because I hate it when she cries.

It's a steeper trail than I thought it would be, but it's glorious at the summit. I have to share the peak with a few other people, but I climb the stairs of the fire tower and have the view all to myself. The sunshine has held out, and all around I see the Adirondacks stretching away in beautiful shades of hazy blue. I wish I could bottle this feeling of making it to the top. Maybe this should be my holy place—every Sunday morning I'll be at the top of a new fire tower, having found my own way to something that actually makes me happy.

It's getting windy (they don't call it Hurricane Mountain for nothing) so I start making my way back down. It's well into the afternoon, and I haven't seen anyone on the trail for some time. I'm trekking along, watching for those trail markers, until it occurs to me that I haven't seen one in a while. The trail is getting a bit rough, too, but it still seems like I'm on some kind of path. Is it the path, though? Again I think of my mom asking if I have a map and swat the memory away like an early mosquito. This has got to be the trail—I'm sure I'll see a marker any minute.

The sun is slanting through the trees with that mellow light that signals early evening. I don't come across a marker, so I reluctantly turn back the way I came, knowing that if I just retrace my steps, I'll get back on the path. I'll walk all the way back up the mountain if I have to. But that will, at best, leave me on the trail long after sunset, and all I've got is the light on my phone. I start to feel a bit anxious, but there's just no way I won't pick up the trail again. It's not like anyone is trying to hide it.

As I resume the climb, I realize I'm following a wash. How long was I doing that? With the mud and melting snow, it's hard to see where my tracks are. I find myself in deep, soft snow, and every step becomes a battle. This doesn't even seem like the way I came down. I fall once and tear my pant leg. I fall a second time, and my ribs find a rock hidden beneath the snow. This knocks the wind out of me, and when I'm doubled over, I realize that I forgot to put the clips on my spikes that keep them from coming undone in deep snow. My brand-new spikes have slipped off and they're somewhere behind me, buried on the darkening mountain. I'm skidding along in worn-out hiking boots, and I still haven't picked up the trail. I am well and truly lost.

I haven't got time to start upbraiding myself about doing such a poor job of preparing. I haven't got a map, and I can't bring one up online because there is no cell service here. I can't even call anyone if I end up needing help. I know there's a pond farther down the trail, and if I come out on the wrong end of that where I can't even get to the footbridge, I'm going to be spending the night on the mountain. It is spring, but with the thin jacket I'm wearing and a small water bottle that's almost empty, it's not going to be a good night. I get a pang of true regret when I think that Mom might be wondering where I am. I didn't tell her what trail I was hiking, for no better reason than that I was in a salty mood. Nobody knows what trail I'm on. I don't even have a job to not show up for tomorrow morning.

There's a creek that runs down the mountain, and I can hear it chattering quietly through the trees. I figure that if I keep following it, I have to get to the bottom, and I'll find the highway, eventually. But for the moment, I'm slipping and sliding through mud and ice, sometimes up to one knee in snow. Ice gets into my pant leg through the tear, and snow has caked around the tops of my boots. My feet are soaking wet. More often than not, I'm pushing my way through saplings and scrambling over fallen trees, and I get more than a few scratches and bruises. This is not the path I had hoped to walk today. I've got to find this trail. I've got to spot a marker, before it gets totally dark, because by the light of my cell phone I will not pick up a three-inch metal disk nailed to a tree. I am more than concerned now. I am pretty sure I won't be getting home tonight. I don't want to think about whether I'll be getting home tomorrow.

My heart leaps when I see a scrap of blue flagging tied around a tree. I heave a shaking sigh of relief; someone else blundered their way down here, too, and wanted to make sure the next idiot found the trail again. With a renewed burst of energy, I slog through the snow. I reach the first bit of flagging, but I can't see anything that looks like the path. I'm still confident, though—I can see another tree in the distance, with another ring of blue around its trunk. What can this be except the way back? I'm almost smiling when I see the third tree, almost jogging along now that the snow isn't so deep. I'm going downhill and I'm sure I'll set foot on the solid, packed snow of the trail at any moment.

Then there are no more marked trees, just the last strip of flagging rattling slightly in the chilly breeze and night falling over me. The western sky is a deep pink above the bare branches, but on the ground I see only ice, mud, snow…and darkness like a mist approaching through the trees from every direction.

I call out, remembering that there were still a couple of hikers at the peak when I left. They must be on their way down by now. I shout until I'm hoarse, but the only answer is the wind whispering around me. You don't realize how big the forest is until you're alone in it at twilight. I have to retrace my steps yet again and stick as close as I can to the creek, because I know—I hope—that it will be my way out.

I'm cursing as I'm struggling across the rough terrain, cursing my own stupidity, cursing the jerk who tied up that flagging to signal nothing, cursing this never-ending trail that is no kind of trail. What in hell made me think hiking in snow would be any fun? Please, I think, please let me get out of here. And then I curse again because I decided months ago that there is no one listening.

That's when I see it. A little red disc, nailed to a tree, with "TRAIL" printed on it in neat white letters. I could kiss it. I see the well-trodden ice. I know it's going to be a slippery trek down, but I am so overjoyed that I don't care how many times I'm going to slip or slide or fall.

After many long minutes of creeping down the trail, I hear a couple of guys behind me. They have headlamps, spikes, hiking poles. Obviously not their first rodeo. They overtake me at the footbridge over the pond. They give me a look as they go by and ask if I'm okay.

"I am now," I answer, and I shiver as I look out over the pond. I can't even see the other end of it in the gloom, and I'm so grateful that I'm not picking my way through the trees that crowd its muddy edges, straining to see the bridge that's now firmly under my feet. "Just lost the trail for a little while," I explain. "Thanks for asking." When they're sure I don't need help, they move on.

It's dark when I get to my car. My ribs are throbbing, and I'm shuffling along like I'm 80 years old. There's only one other car in the parking lot—those two guys have hung around to make sure I get off the trail. It seems in that moment like the greatest kindness anyone's ever done for me. I give them a wave in thanks as their headlights sweep across me, and the driver taps his horn as they speed off down Highway Nine. I'm left alone, and the stars are coming out. I don't think I've ever felt such relief, such gratitude, such exhaustion. I have an extra water bottle in my car, and I down it in about three gulps. I still have a two-hour drive ahead, but I need a few deep breaths before I pull onto the road. Maybe I'll stop in Saranac Lake for a snooze.

I make that stop, but it's to call my mom. Hopefully she hasn't been worrying, because it's not like she was expecting another call today—she trusted me when I said it was just a little half-day hike on a popular trail. I only mean to tell her that I'm on my way home, but she can hear that I don't sound quite right, and I end up telling her the whole story.

"I'm glad you're safe." She talks a little too loud, as if volume will steady that wobble her voice gets when she's trying not to cry. "Make sure you stop again if you feel sleepy."

"I will." This time I'm not annoyed that she has reminded me of something I already know. I just feel glad I'm hearing her voice from inside a warm car next to a brightly lit gas station.

"Come on over when you get back to the city, even though it'll be late," she urges. "I'll make you some supper. You've had a hard day."

"Okay." No rebukes; she's not that way. She just wants to see me and give me something good to eat. "I'm sorry I didn't tell you exactly where I was going."

"It's all right now. You'll know for next time."

We end the call and I get back on the road, but pretty soon I have to stop again. It's not that I can't keep my eyes open, but that they are filling with tears. I think about Mom and Millie. I think about Sunday mornings and a sink full of dirty coffee cups. I think about the long road ahead, and how it is not only on the mountain that I am following the washes down into the dark.

PILGRIMAGE TO L5

Karina Fabian

The hard wood of the kneeler pressed against eight-year-old Lucy Granger's knees as she knelt for Communion prayers. She cracked her eyes open. Stained glass told the story of Jesus but hid the stars. Statues of saints looked on over electric candles. The priest raised the Host—and he didn't float or anything.

She sighed. A space church should look more spacey!

Mom had lied. She'd said moving to Mars would be exciting, but all the "Kids' Fun" stuff on the *Sebastien* had gotten old weeks ago. Mostly, they were stuck in a boring little stateroom, where all Mom did was read stuff for her new job and stare at Papa's picture and pretend she wasn't crying.

They were getting one day to visit L5, the biggest space station in the system. It had a zero-g amusement park! Papa would have taken her to the park, tossed her in the zero-g tank, and laughed. She wanted to go laugh for him, but Mom wanted to tour a church.

"Honestly, Lucy! Do you have any idea how lucky we are?" her mother entreated. "How many people can say they visited the home of Saint Gillian—on the one-year anniversary of her sainthood, even? It's a pilgrimage. We'll get blessings."

It was the most excited she'd seen Mom all trip. They probably needed extra blessings with Papa gone, so Lucy forced a smile and said it'd be fun, too.

Maybe it could have been. Saint Gillian had founded the Rescue Sisters: nuns who did exciting search and rescue operations in space. But the convent was just an arm of the station, Saint Gillian's "home" was a closet, and after the information video, they went to church where her mom kept wiping her eyes.

Churches were boring. And sad.

I'm tired of being bored and sad, she thought, casting her eyes upward. God, couldn't something exciting happen?

At that moment, her mom nudged her, and she took her place in line for Communion.

"The life of a Rescue Sister, like so many of those in space, is long periods of tedium and routine punctuated by times of excitement—which can mean high stress and danger," Sister Mary Elizabeth said to the group as they entered the common room.

The thirty-or-so pilgrims turned this way and that, looking around with interest. Lucy didn't know why. It was just computers and tables and doors to other rooms. If not for the religious art (and the fact that you could see the pipes in the ceiling), it could have been the common room on the *Sebastien*.

Sister Mary Elizabeth continued, "So it's important that every sister stay engaged, not just spiritually, but also physically and mentally. Here is where we do most of our studying—whether on the lives of the saints or the latest medical technologies. The rooms behind you hold our classroom and our flight simulator. The simulator can be adjusted to resemble any of our ships, and we sometimes train station pilots here as well. To the front of us is the gym and the splat court—"

"You play splat?" her mother exclaimed.

Lucy's ears perked up. Splat was a sport designed specifically for zero gravity, a cross between basketball and full-contact rugby as the teams tried to keep each other from making a point in any way possible. Papa had let her watch a game with him, but Mama said it was too violent.

And the sisters played it for fun?

Sister Mary Elizabeth laughed. "We get our share of bruises. But it's a great way to develop the reflexes and zero-g movements that we sometimes need in a rescue. That said, it's not a required sport. However, we do insist on—"

Suddenly, something leaped from the pipes in the ceiling and landed on Sister's back.

A woman in the front screamed, but Sister merely snickered. "There you are, Gabriel! Who's a good kitty?"

She leaned her head to one side and Gabriel obligingly rubbed his cheek against hers.

"This is Gabriel. He's a special breed of cat, adapted for space stations and ships. You can see his paws have long toes for gripping, and his tail is strong like a monkey's. This makes it easier for him to move in low or no gravity. He understands some basic commands, including 'Come' and 'Fetch.' Cats play an important role on a station like this, where it's easy for vermin to sneak aboard items coming from Earth."

As if knowing his moment was over, Gabriel jumped off Sister Mary Elizabeth's shoulders and sauntered across a table.

"If you'll follow me into the gym, Sister Cassandra is going to do a demonstration of our standard exercise routine..."

Lucy barely listened as Sister explained something about combining prayer and exercise. Gabriel was sitting on a keyboard, staring at her with big, green eyes. She waited as people filed past her, her mother included, making their way to the gym.

Then she held out her hand. "Kitty, kitty... Can you shake hands? Shake?"

Gabriel regarded her hand with a cat's usual disdain, yawned, and leaped off the table. He sauntered toward the open door Sister had not explained.

Then he paused and looked at her.

"You want me to follow?"

With tail held high and an attitude that he didn't really care, he started down the corridor.

Lucy followed, and when the cat turned and went through an open hatch, so did she—and found herself inside one of the actual ships the sisters used for rescues.

Now, this was interesting!

Sister Gemma greeted Sister Thérèse in the common room with a sardonic smile. "Ready to go perform for the tourists?"

Sister Thérèse's jaw dropped, and she said in a whisper. "Sister! They're not tourists; they're pilgrims."

"Then they should be praying."

Together, the two started toward the shuttle.

"They did pray. Now, they get to see what we do. I mean, we don't spend all day praying, or we wouldn't earn our air. Besides, we have to train somehow."

"Which is why you're in charge today," Sister Gemma told her. "Is the shuttle prepped?"

"Yep. I already did pre-flight. Even lubricated the interior doors. We can respond as soon as Freddy gives the signal." Freddy had volunteered to simulate an EVA emergency—being thrown from the station without his safety line—and the sisters would swoop in and pick him up. It was a standard exercise for certification but impressive to the gravfeets watching from the observation deck. To make things interesting, L5 had tossed out some large pieces of broken equipment for Sister Thérèse to maneuver around.

They entered the shuttle and almost tripped on Gabriel, who howled and dashed out.

"Gabes!" Sister Gemma shouted, then laughed. "That cat is more trouble!"

An alert signal sounded.

"Here we go. Your orders, Sister?"

Sister Thérèse blinked. "Oh! Um, secure the airlock, and I'll get the engines going. Once you buckle in, we're off."

"Before that?" Sister Gemma prompted.

She smiled at her trainer. How could she forget? "We pray, of course!"

Lucy had spent a fascinated few minutes staring at the cockpit controls, wondering what the different buttons and levers meant and feeling a growing desire to find out. Then, she heard voices in the corridor coming her way!

Her mother would kill her—or worse, ground her until they reached Mars. She ran back toward the hatch, realized the only way out was past the approaching nuns, and scanned the area for a place to hide.

There! A closet. She smacked a button, and the hatch opened with amazing quiet. She jumped into the tiny space and shut the door just as she heard Gabriel crash into one of the nuns. Good kitty!

Maureen Granger wound her way to the front of the group and watched in rapt attention as a sister demonstrated the exercise machines and Sister Mary Elizabeth explained how the prayers were patterned for targeted breathing. Maybe Maureen could start doing this herself.

Thank you for this opportunity, Lord. Thank you that Lucy was okay with it. Maureen knew her daughter would have preferred the distraction of fun, but Maureen needed this—a chance for worship that wasn't tainted by the funeral, by people looking at her with sad eyes, telling her, "Trust God," in that vague way people did. She'd needed to see other women living in that trust—betting their very lives on it. Maybe then, she'd see her way forward without Gary.

Sister Mary Elizabeth's voice broke through her brooding. "Now if everyone will join me in the observation lounge, we're going to demonstrate a rescue for you."

"How exciting! Did you hear that, Lucy?" Maureen turned to her daughter but did not find her. "Lucy? Has anyone seen my daughter?"

Lucy blinked in the darkness. It was absolutely silent. How would she know when it was safe to go?

I'll count to a hundred, then peek, she decided.

She got to 75 when suddenly the room shook, and her feet rose from the floor.

We're moving? Panicked, she started slapping the door screaming, "I'm in here! Help!"

Her hands scrambled for the lock. She found a button, pushed it. The lights came on.

Suddenly, she was pressed hard against the door.

Suddenly, she was pressed hard against the door.

The shuttle gave a small lurch, and a warning light came on.

"The escape pod jettisoned," Sister Gemma reported, her voice bland.

Sister Thérèse felt the reproach, nonetheless. "How? I checked it! It…" Biting back a useless protest, she tapped the comms. "*St. Jude* to L5. Be advised that we've lost an escape pod. Can you—"

Suddenly proximity alarms blared, and the automatic controls activated. The ship lurched as braking jets fired. A large piece of space trash sailed past their viewscreen. Moments later, they heard thumps, like rainfall on a steel roof, as debris peppered the side of their ship.

Overtop the noise, L5 was saying the escape pod had smacked into a piece of debris in the field, causing a chain reaction. The pod itself was in a tumble and heading toward Mars.

Inside the closet, all Lucy could do was scream as she got tossed from one part of the room to another, smacking a wall or piece of equipment before getting shoved back against the door. Then the pressure eased and she started floating, and she had to stop screaming because her stomach was doing flips.

"Don't throw up. It'll be gross," a voice said.

With a yelp, she turned—or tried to. The effort sent her spinning and tumbling. Somehow, she grabbed a handle in the wall and stopped herself.

Chairs? Controls? This wasn't a closet—it was an escape pod!

Her lunch tried to climb up her throat.

A little holographic figure of a woman in a Rescue Sisters "habit"—black T-shirt and loose pants over a spacer's skinsuit—and the reddest hair she'd ever seen floated between the chairs. It looked like Saint Gillian.

The hologram pointed to a pocket by the chair. "There's a sickbag in the—"

Lucy was already scrabbling for the bag, her arms windmilling and legs flailing. She got it to her mouth just in time.

When her stomach had emptied itself and she could breathe again, she started to cry.

"How can she be gone?" Maureen cried. "She was just here!"

Sister Mary Elizabeth rubbed Maureen's arms and spoke reassuringly. They were in the common room, the others searching while she comforted her. "She can't have gone far. Could she be hiding from us, perhaps?"

"No, no. She wouldn't. She knows..." Maureen paused to sob. "It's just us. We have to stick together. It's just us."

Gabriel hopped up on the chair and weaseled his way onto her lap.

One of the pilgrims looked their way. "Hey, I saw the kid talking to the cat. Maybe she followed him somewhere?"

"Wonderful idea." Sister Mary Elizabeth used her wrist comms to let the other sisters know to look where Gabey had last been seen.

Suddenly, alarms rang throughout the room, announcing a genuine emergency, outside, in the demo area.

Mother Superior entered the room and clapped her hands sharply. "Everyone! Please, let's head back to the chapel."

"What?" Maureen exclaimed. "What about Lucy?"

"We'll keep searching. The chapel is safest for guests," Mother Superior said. "You can pray for her and for the rescue there."

"Rescue?" The word made no sense. "But Lucy—"

Sister Mary Elizabeth lifted Gabriel from Maureen's lap and helped her stand up. Maureen leaned on her as they walked.

"Don't worry, Maureen. We'll find her. Trust God."

Maureen froze. Trust God? When her daughter, all that was left of the man she'd loved, was God-only-knew where? Trust Him? "How?"

"Faith, hope, and love."

"'Faith, hope, and love?' What does that mean?" Lucy sniffled. She hurt everywhere and her stomach was gurgly, but crying wouldn't help. It never did. So she swallowed hard and tried to listen to the hologram.

St. Gillian gave her a matter-of-fact smile. "Faith is one foot in the air, one in a crook, and a queasy feeling in your gut. See that U-shaped bar on the floor? That's a crook. Can you sneak your foot in it?"

It took a few tries, and she almost got sick again, but eventually she did it. "Okay—but I don't understand."

"Even when something is hard or scary—makes our tummies hurt—faith gives us the strength to cling to our support while we move forward. Now, let's see about that tummy. Did you know the Rescue Sisters have a special prayer they say in free fall to help with nausea? If you say it right, it soothes the stomach and the soul. Now, all in one breath: Jesus Savior…"

It took some fancy flying, but Sister Thérèse managed to pilot the Saint *Jude* away from the wildly careening debris. Meanwhile, Sister Gemma ensured that Freddy, the spacer they were to "rescue," was fine, checked for damage, and reported back to L5.

"You got lucky," the dispatcher said. "That escape pod went flying smack into the center of the debris, sending things scattering like pool balls. Things are still colliding and busting up. No more making things exciting for the tourists! Trash catchers are deploying. Hey, Sister Emmie wants to know if you saw Gabriel before launch. Guess there's a kid missing, and she might have followed him?"

The two sisters shared horrified looks. The escape pod!

While Sister Thérèse relayed their suspicions, Sister Gemma tried to reach the pod. "No luck. The radio must be damaged."

"And who knows what else?" Sister Thérèse bit back panic. "I should have checked that the pod was empty!"

"As should I," Sister Gemma said, her hands working the controls, already making calculations for speed, reaction fuel, and other data they'd need to chase the pod. "Let's stow the self-recrimination."

"Copy. Saint *Jude* to Freddy. We have to get the escape pod, then we'll be back—"

Her explanation was cut off by a scream and alerts from Freddy's suit. He'd been hit by debris.

"She's *where*?" Maureen shouted. She jerked away from Sister Mary Elizabeth and wildly scanned the walls, looking for any peek to the outside that might reveal her baby. Biblical characters in stained glass mocked her anxiety. She spun toward the exit, every part of her screaming to run—but where? She couldn't run to Lucy in the middle of space. She couldn't do anything.

She turned back to the older nun who had delivered the news. "Help her!"

"We are," Mother Superior said. "We're launching the *Archangel Michael*—"

"Launching? What about the ship that's already out there?"

"The spacer outside was injured—" Mother Superior started, but people had gathered.

One man asked, "So there's a real emergency? Can we watch?"

Watch? Her baby was hurtling toward Mars, and they wanted a show? "What about Lucy?" Maureen shouted.

Sister Mary Elizabeth rubbed her shoulders reassuringly. "The *Michael* will get her. She'll be fine."

"Are you sure?" She took a breath. *Calm down.* "So the pod's okay? You contacted her?"

When neither Rescue Sister answered immediately, Maureen wailed and fell against Sister Mary Elizabeth's shoulder.

"I can't lose her! What do I do?"

Sister Mary Elizabeth pulled away to look at her directly. "We're going to rescue her. That's our job. Your job is to hope and to pray. Faith, hope, and love. Have faith in us. Have faith in God. Hope for her safe return. And pray with all the love you have."

"Am I going to die?" Lucy asked the hologram of Saint Gillian. She had said the free fall prayer twice and her stomach was calmer, but outside the porthole was nothing but stars. Saint Gillian had told her how to use the radio on the wall beside her, but it didn't work. Plus, she was getting cold. She was starting to see her breath, and that seemed wrong for a spaceship.

St. Gillian laughed. "You are a dramatic little thing, aren't you? Where's your hope? You know what hope is, right?"

"Hope reminds us that God is in control and everything has a purpose," she muttered. She remembered because Father had said it at Papa's funeral, and it didn't make sense. What purpose was there to her papa dying? Now, they were going to Mars without him. It wasn't fair.

"You miss your daddy," Saint Gillian said softly.

Without wondering how the hologram knew, Lucy nodded.

"That's the hardest part about being human. People die, and it's awful, and sometimes it doesn't make sense. We don't get to see the universe like God does. That makes hope harder than faith. Your daddy loves you very much, even now, and he's proud of you."

"He'd be mad. I was naughty and ran off," Lucy said. She felt the tears coming, so she took in a cold breath and repeated the prayer Saint Gillain had taught her. *Jesus Savior...*

"You're very brave," Saint Gillian said. "Apologize and take your punishment later, and he'll be proud of how grown-up you're being."

"He used to call me 'Little Lady,'" Lucy said.

"Tell me more," Saint Gillian urged, and Lucy did.

Even with her flying skills, Sister Thérèse could not get the Saint *Jude* close enough to catch Freddy with the net. Even worse, he'd lost consciousness.

The viewscreen showed a growing cloud of smaller objects, some still bumping into each other to create even more. She'd long since turned off the proximity alarm, relying on the viewscreen to show dangers in flashing red. Freddy himself floated in a cloud of frozen oxygen and blood.

Sister Thérèse tried not to think about it.

"This is the best I can do," she said as she hit the reverse thrusters to stop their momentum.

"It'll work," Sister Gemma said over the comms. She was already suiting up in the back. Sister Thérèse was supposed to have done the EVA, but given the danger, Gemma, who had fifteen years more experience, was the best choice to go after Freddy. "We were going to have to work around some space junk, anyway."

"But that was big stuff for the tourists to see! Now there's so much and it's moving and..." As if to emphasize her point, the hull thumped as something bounced off it. Automatically, she compensated to keep the ship in place.

But all Gemma said was, "'Tourists'?"

She laughed without humor. "You know what I mean. I should have checked the pod, or told you to check. Now Freddy's hurt and Saint *Jude*'s damaged and we had to send the *Michael* after the girl and who knows if she—"

"That's enough, Sister," Sister Gemma scolded. "Faith, hope, and love. Where are they?"

It was a calming exercise of the sisters. Sister Thérèse answered, "Faith in God's providence and the skills of my sisters, hope for successful rescues, love as the force that connects us and the blanket of calm in my heart. You're right. I'm okay. Are you ready?"

"Opening the airlock. The way looks pretty clear. Well done, Sister. Heading out."

Sister Thérèse already had a screen showing the view outside the airlock. "I see you." Yet even though she kept an eye on Sister Gemma, ready to call out any dangers of debris floating her way, part of her mind was on the small child alone in the vastness of space. Was she hurt?

She must be so scared.

"I'm not scared," Lucy told the hologram, "at least, not anymore. I just hurt all over, and I'm cold and a little dizzy."

"Are you?" Saint Gillian asked. "I'm sorry. There's a blanket in that panel to your right. Yes, there. Then come curl up in a chair."

"I don't want to take my foot out of the crook!" Saint Gillian had said the crook was faith and if she let go...

She knew she was being stupid, but she felt if she didn't keep one foot anchored, she'd cry all over again.

"It's alright," the hologram soothed. "Seatbelts are a good crook, too. And there's a heater in the seat."

That sparked her to action, and after some awkward scrambling and bumping her elbow and shin, she managed to settle into one of the seats, the heater on and the blanket tucked around her.

"Do I need to keep a foot in the air?"

"No, dear. You're showing great faith, and hope, too. That leaves love. Do you know what love is?"

Lucy hadn't realized how cold she was. Now that she was warming up, it was hard to think. She shrugged. "Love just is. I love Papa. I love Mommy."

"Love means to will the good of another. Right now, lots of people are willing good things for you. Everyone's praying for your rescue. The sisters are coming as fast as they can. And your mother is praying with all the love in her heart. So just feel their love, like a blanket over your heart. Do you feel it?"

She nodded. "I feel sleepy."

"I know, but don't sleep yet. Tell me about the people you love. How do you will good for them?"

"I love Mommy." Lucy hitched the blanket a little higher over her ears. "I guess the good I want is for her to be happy again." She sniffled. "Bet she's crying."

"Sometimes, we cry before we can laugh. It's in the Bible: *Those who sow in tears shall reap with shouts of joy.*"

"I'm too tired to shout."

"Stay awake. Who else do you love?"

Those who sow in tears shall reap with shouts of joy.

Maureen blinked and lifted her head from where it had been pressed against her clasped hands. Who had said that? It must have been one of the sisters. Still, when she glanced around, she didn't see any nearby. Everyone else, having finished a Rosary, had gathered around someone's handheld, cheering over the rescue. The spacer's, not Lucy's.

She was alone.

She pressed her forehead against her thumbs again. *I am sowing. I have been for months. I'm sowing, and I may never shout for joy again.*

Faith, hope, and love. Amen, amen, I say to you, you will weep and mourn, while the world rejoices; you will grieve, but your grief will become joy, came the answer.

I want to have joy, she answered back. *If only for Lucy. She's so young; she deserves a life with joy. Bring her back to me, please God! Bring her back, and I promise to let you lead me back to joy.*

She didn't hear an answer, but Maureen felt a weight, like a warm blanket being draped over her shoulders. The comfort seeped through her, and while her tears still flowed, the knot in her stomach loosened.

Her mind began to wander. She saw Gary's face and prayed for his soul—something she hadn't done since the shock had worn off and the depression had closed in. She thought of all her friends, with their sad eyes and hesitant looks, and prayed thanksgiving that they'd tried to be there for her. She prayed for her Little Lucy, so brave and curious, and for the sisters on the *Archangel Michael*—

A hand gently grasped her shoulder. "Maureen?" Sister Mary Elizabeth said. "They found her. She's alright. They're bringing her home."

Freddy was groggy but conscious by the time the Saint *Jude* docked. As the medical team wheeled him out, he grabbed Sister Gemma's arm.

He pulled off his oxygen mask. "Did the tourists enjoy the show?"

Sister Gemma scowled at him. "They're pilgrims, and they were busy praying for you."

He chuckled as she put his mask back on.

Sister Thérèse wondered how he could laugh about all this. *Will I ever have that level of zed?*

Not today, she decided as Sister Gemma motioned her back into the ship. They had cleanup, and of course, her evaluation.

She decided she could not stand the wait. "Okay, Sister, just tell me. How much retraining am I in for?"

Sister Gemma paused in wiping her helmet. "Pardon?"

"I jettisoned this eval! I didn't check for stowaways; I'm responsible for an accident that injured one person and left a huge mess outside; and you had to talk me down in the middle of a rescue!"

Sister Gemma finished hanging her suit and sat across from her trainee. "True enough, but missing that girl was on both of us—and there's no procedure about checking the escape pod immediately prior to launch. We need new rules now that we have more people visiting the convent. The mess was bad luck, but you piloted us around it like a champ. As for the moment of doubt... It happens to the best of us. It takes practice to put fear and self-recrimination aside until the mission is done. You'll get there, and you recovered quickly. I think Saint Gillian would be proud."

Sister Thérèse slumped with relief. "Really?"

"Faith, hope, and love. We just have to trust that this is all in God's plan."

Maureen did indeed cry with joy when they carried Lucy out of the *Archangel Michael*, wrapped in a mylar blanket and looking more sleepy than injured. Maureen tore away from Sister Mary Elizabeth and Mother Superior and ran to greet the team. She cried again as they transferred Lucy into her arms.

Gabriel, the cat, sauntered past the sisters and started rubbing against Maureen's legs, purring.

"My baby! Oh, my sweet baby." Maureen kissed Lucy's cheeks and hair.

"Mommy! I'm sorry. I didn't mean to—"

"It doesn't matter. You're here. You're okay." Then she paused to look at the sister who'd been carrying her. "She is okay?"

The sister nodded with a smile. "A few bumps and bruises, some hypothermia—smart girl, finding the blanket and heater. A touch of hypercapnia—that's too much carbon dioxide in her system. But the tri-ox should clear that up soon enough."

"She gave me a shot!" Lucy complained.

Maureen laughed. It felt good to laugh. "My brave baby! You must have been so scared, alone in that pod."

"Uh-uh!" She shook her head, then reconsidered. "Maybe at first—but Saint Gillian took care of me."

"Saint Gillian?" She looked over her daughter's head at the sisters, who shrugged.

"Yeah. The hologram. She told me what to do and talked to me about Papa and you, and she told me stories. She said to have faith, hope, and love. 'Faith is one foot in the crook, one in the air, and your stomach all queasy.'"

Lucy laid her head more comfortably on her mother's shoulder.

Maureen cradled it with one hand, but her attention was caught by the wide-eyed looks the sisters were sharing. Sister Mary Elizabeth brought her hands to her mouth, and her eyes swam with tears.

Lucy murmured, "I liked that hologram. Can we get a copy? She's nice."

"I think," the Mother Superior said, "that we need to take you over to the infirmary for a thorough checkup and get you something warm. Do you like hot chocolate?"

With the bribe of cocoa, Lucy let herself be carried by the sister from the ship. As the Rescue Sister took Lucy to the infirmary, she asked her about the hologram. Gabriel trotted after them.

Sister Mary Elizabeth and Mother Superior held Maureen back, however.

"What's wrong?" she asked, clenching her teeth against fear. *No more, God! I just got her back.*

But Mother Superior asked, "How much does she know about Saint Gillian? The Rescue Sisters?"

Maureen shrugged. "Just what we learned today. I'm sorry. I guess I'm not the best Catholic. Why?"

"There's no hologram on the rescue pod," Mother Superior said.

"But…"

Sister Mary Elizabeth clasped her wrist. She looked ready to leap with excitement. "And what she said about faith? It's one of Saint Gillian's favorite sayings, but very few know it outside the Sisters—even most Spacers don't."

"We've never heard it. I don't understand. What are you saying—she imagined it all?"

Mother Superior answered. "That's why I want her thoroughly examined and questioned. It could be she heard it somewhere—"

Sister Mary Elizabeth jumped in. "But it's equally possible that it was the real Saint Gillian. It's happened before. It happened to me."

Maureen shivered, thinking of the voice she'd heard: *Faith, hope, and love.*

She'd received her blessing. She saw the way forward.

FAITHFUL JOURNEYS, HIDDEN SANCTUARIES

John Ruberto

Richmond, North Yorkshire, 1577

Thomas Owen rubbed beeswax into the oak wood, filling the room with a warm, honey-sweet aroma, as Sir William Gascoigne stepped into the bedchamber.

"Magnificent craftsmanship," said William, running his hand along the curved edge of the largest wardrobe. "This cabinet is exquisite—the joinery so precise you can scarcely see the seams. The roses on the panels, a work of art. My wife will be overjoyed."

"Thank you, Sir William; your compliments mean much to me, and credit goes to my helper, Nicholas."

"When we met all those years ago in Walsingham, back when you called me Bill, you wished for a child. Now, your grandson is your traveling companion. What a world we live in."

Glancing at his grandson, Thomas said, "Show Sir William your drawer."

Hiding a smirk and trying to appear serious, Nicholas opened the middle drawer and said, "See, I placed my shirt in this drawer. Once I remove the shirt, the bottom looks normal. But, if you slide this rose here, it unlatches the drawer bottom." Nicholas lifted the false bottom, revealing the hidden compartment.

William tousled the boy's hair, then reached into his jacket pocket, took out an envelope and placed it into the secret hiding spot. "This is exactly what we needed," he said before leaving to find his wife. On his way out, he said, "Oh, Thomas, that letter is for you. It arrived this morning."

Thomas retrieved the letter from the false drawer bottom and read it with a frown. "I have ill tidings, Nicholas. Your mother..." His voice broke. "She was caught attending a secret Mass at the Harts.' They killed her. And the others."

Nicholas blinked, not understanding the words that his grandfather had uttered. He snatched the letter from his grandfather's hands. His brow furrowed as he read the letter. "This cannot be. A just God would not take her from me. When did this happen?"

"The letter is dated four weeks past. We left Oxford five weeks ago."

The York Road

Thomas guided the horses and wagon around another muddy hollow in the road. Three days had passed since they had left Richmond behind, as he glanced sideways at his grandson, whose eyes remained fixed on some distant point beyond the horizon.

Nicholas had barely spoken three sentences since receiving news of his mother's passing. His slender fingers, usually so dexterous with tools, now merely twisted a small wooden cross he had received years earlier—a gift from his mother.

"York should be visible once we crest that hill," Thomas said, hoping to draw the boy from his silence.

Nicholas didn't respond, his lips pressed into a thin line. When he finally spoke, his voice was rough with disuse. "What's the point of going to Walsingham?"

"The shrine building may be gone, but the place remains sacred," Thomas replied softly.

"Sacred?" Nicholas spat bitterly. "Where was this sacred power when my mother lay dying? What good is faith when it doesn't protect those who believe?"

Thomas let the outburst hang in the air between them, watching as his grandson angrily wiped away a tear. The boy's grief was still raw, a fresh wound that no words could immediately heal.

"I was once like you," Thomas said after a long pause. "Full of rage at God. Your grandmother, Agnes, and I had some troubles after we wed. They felt like a betrayal."

Nicholas looked up, surprise momentarily replacing the anger in his eyes. "What type of trouble?"

"We tried for years to have a child. Each month that passed without her womb quickening felt like God's judgment," Thomas replied. "For years, I carried that anger like you do now—a fire in my soul. I questioned why God would grant children to the wicked yet deny them to us who kept the faith in secret. I feared Him but couldn't love Him."

The wagon crested the hill, revealing the distant walls of York and the towering spire of the Minster catching the morning light.

"So, what changed?" Nicholas asked, his voice smaller now, vulnerable.

"My pilgrimage to Walsingham," Thomas said. "I went with your grandmother because my employer demanded it, not because I believed. I walked those miles cursing under my breath, determined to remain unmoved. That is where we met Sir William."

Nicholas leaned forward; his attention caught despite himself.

"But something happened to me there—something I still cannot fully explain with words," Thomas continued. "In that Holy House, as I knelt before Our Lady, I heard a voice—whether from within my heart or truly from her lips, I cannot say—telling me Agnes would bear my child. Within months of returning home, your father was conceived. It wasn't about getting the answer I wanted, Nicholas. It was about finding peace in surrendering to God's timing."

"What questions should I be asking, then?" Nicholas challenged, though with less heat than before.

Thomas smiled gently. "That, my boy, is why we're making this journey together. Some questions can only be answered by the road itself."

Nicholas looked away, but Thomas noticed he had stopped twisting the wooden cross and was now holding it still in his palm, his thumb tracing its contours with something akin to care.

York

"We are seeking Margaret Clitherow. Her husband is a butcher in the Shambles," Thomas told his grandson. "She is careful of strangers, but Sir William gave us this letter of introduction. She is known to the magistrates for more than once refusing to attend Anglican services. Some admire her courage; others—others condemn her defiance."

Thomas guided the horse and wagon to the Shambles, its narrow lane crowded with timber-framed buildings that leaned toward each other until their upper stories nearly touched. Butchers' shops lined the cobbled street, their wooden counters jutting out beneath wide windows where meat was displayed and sold to passing customers. The sweet-copper scent of blood mingled with the sawdust strewn across the stones.

"This is it," Thomas said, stopping before a shop midway down the lane. Above the entrance hung a painted sign depicting a cleaver and side of beef.

Nicholas noted how ordinary it looked—indistinguishable from the dozen other butcher shops they'd passed. No one would suspect that behind this unremarkable façade lay a sanctuary for the forbidden faith.

A woman looked up from behind the counter as they entered. She was sturdy rather than slender, with an open, honest face and clear eyes that assessed them quickly. Despite her simple dress, Nicholas sensed her quiet authority.

After reading the letter, Margaret said, "Master Owen, I hope Sir William is well. And this must be your grandson."

"Indeed, he is well, Mistress Clitherow," Thomas replied with a slight bow. "This is Nicholas."

Margaret smiled at Nicholas, but her eyes held a touch of sadness. "I am sorry to hear about your mother. May her soul rest in peace."

"Thank you," Nicholas managed, the familiar ache surfacing again at the mention of his loss.

Margaret turned and called through the door at the back of the shop. "Anne! Mind the counter for a while." A girl of about twelve appeared, wiping her hands on her apron. "These are friends," Margaret told her. "We'll be upstairs."

They followed her through the back of the shop and up a narrow staircase to the living quarters above.

"John is at the market," Margaret explained, gesturing for them to sit at a table by the window. "The little ones are with my mother today." She poured them each a cup of small beer from a pitcher. "Now, what brings a master carpenter and his apprentice to my humble home?"

Thomas leaned forward, lowering his voice despite being away from public ears. "We're journeying to Walsingham. I've been there before, many years ago, but Nicholas needs to see it—even in its ruined state."

Margaret's face softened with understanding. "Ah, Walsingham." She shook her head slowly. "It's not what it was, Thomas. Henry's men were thorough in their destruction. The Holy House is gone, the statues smashed, the treasures stolen." She looked at Nicholas. "What do you hope to find there, young man?"

Nicholas stared into his cup. "I'm not certain," he admitted. "My grandfather believes it might help me... understand some things."

"Faith is a precious thing in these times," Margaret said softly. "Easily broken, not so easily mended." She reached across the table to touch Thomas's hand. "But you are welcome to rest here before continuing your journey. In fact, you might find additional comfort here tonight."

Thomas's eyebrows raised in question.

"Father William arrives this afternoon," Margaret said, her voice barely above a whisper. "Disguised as a wool merchant. We'll have Mass after dark. You are welcome to join us."

Nicholas looked up sharply. He hadn't attended a proper Mass in weeks—the risk was too great in the small villages where strangers were noticed immediately.

"We would be honored," Thomas replied.

Margaret stood. "Good. Now, let me show you something."

She led them to the hearth, kneeling beside it. With practiced movements, she pressed a particular stone in the fireplace surround. A section of the hearth floor swung upward, revealing a shallow compartment beneath.

"When Father William celebrates Mass," she explained, "we lay a board here across the opening. The chalice sits upon it, and should there be a raid, everything can be hidden in seconds."

Nicholas knelt beside her, examining the mechanism with professional interest. "The pivot is clever," he said, demonstrating how the stone released the catch.

Later, a linen merchant rang the bell of the Clitherow house. Quickly ushering the merchant into the house, Margaret said, "Welcome Father William. Two more for our congregation tonight."

The priest nodded warmly to the carpenters. "Welcome, brothers. God's peace be with you."

The main room had been transformed. Heavy curtains covered the windows, and several candles provided the only light. A small group of people—perhaps ten in all—sat quietly on benches and chairs arranged to face the hearth. At their center stood a man in simple merchant's clothing, his travel-worn appearance belying the calm authority in his bearing.

As they took seats at the back, Nicholas watched in fascination as Margaret and two other women completed the preparations. Just as she had shown them earlier, the board was placed over the hearth compartment. From beneath it, Margaret withdrew a chalice wrapped in fine linen, a small silver paten, and a wooden crucifix so well-carved that Nicholas immediately recognized the hand of a master craftsman.

The items were arranged reverently on the makeshift altar, and a small, leather-bound missal appeared from another hiding place. Candles were positioned carefully, their light reflecting off the silver chalice and casting long shadows across the room.

Father William donned a simple stole that had been concealed in the folds of his cloak. As he began to speak the ancient Latin words, Nicholas felt an unexpected tightness in his throat. How many times had he heard these same phrases, standing beside his mother in better days? How many times had he taken the ritual for granted?

"In nomine Patris, et Filii, et Spiritus Sancti..."

King's Lynn

Two weeks after leaving York, they arrived at Master Henry Dawson's estate in King's Lynn, bearing a sealed letter of introduction from Margaret Clitherow.

"Watch your step here," said Dawson, pressing against an unassuming wooden panel in his library. The bookcase swung silently outward, revealing a narrow opening. "The space beyond can hold two men, though it would be a tight fit for more."

Nicholas peered into the darkness of the priest hole with undisguised fascination. The craftsmanship was impressive—the seams nearly invisible, the hinges silent, the latch ingeniously simple.

"May I?" Nicholas asked, gesturing to the opening.

Master Dawson nodded. "By all means."

Nicholas ducked through the narrow entrance, immediately assessing the construction with a craftsman's eye. The space was perhaps five feet deep and three feet wide, with a low ceiling. A small bench had been built into one wall, and an air vent disguised as part of the exterior stonework.

"The release mechanism is different from anything I've seen," Nicholas called out, his voice slightly muffled. His finger traced along a joint where the wood met stone, his brow furrowing slightly.

Nicholas emerged from the priest hole, his eyes alight with professional admiration, though something in his expression suggested he was troubled by a detail he'd observed.

"How long would someone need to hide in there?" he asked.

"Once, Father Edmund remained concealed for three days while pursuivants searched the house and grounds." Dawson glanced toward the windows.

"May I make some measurements?" Nicholas asked, already reaching for his drawing implements.

While Nicholas sketched, Thomas and Dawson discussed the increasing dangers facing Catholics.

"They took Edward Johnson last month," Dawson said. "A good man with five children. His only crime was harboring a priest who baptized his newborn daughter."

Nicholas, though focused on his sketches, couldn't help overhearing. The dangers suddenly felt more immediate than they ever had in his father's workshop.

"The trigger mechanism is clever," Nicholas said, pressing the panel as Dawson had shown him. The bookcase swung open, but Nicholas frowned. "I fear it might be too simple and could be opened by accident."

Thomas placed a hand on his grandson's shoulder. "Perhaps that talent of yours serves a higher purpose than merely crafting fine furniture, Nicholas."

Looking up from his sketches, Nicholas met his grandfather's gaze. For the first time, he considered that his skills might have a more vital use—one that could mean the difference between life and death for people like the Dawsons, like Margaret Clitherow, and like the nameless priests who moved through England's shadows.

"I'd like to understand more about how these hiding places are constructed," Nicholas said.

As the afternoon light slanted through the windows, Nicholas filled page after page with drawings, his grief temporarily set aside as his mind engaged with a puzzle that seemed, for the first time since his mother's death, worthy of his full attention. Craftsmanship, he was beginning to understand, could be an act of faith itself.

Walsingham

The ruins of Walsingham Abbey rose before them, a skeletal remnant of former glory caught in the late afternoon light. Only the east wall still stood to any height, its empty window frames like hollow eyes staring across the deserted grounds. Weeds grew between fallen stones, and sheep grazed where pilgrims once knelt in prayer.

Thomas halted the wagon at the edge of the former outer courtyard. For a long moment, he sat motionless, his weathered hands gripping the reins so tightly his knuckles whitened. His face, which had remained stoic through their entire journey, suddenly crumpled.

"Grandfather?" Nicholas reached out, alarmed by the older man's reaction.

Thomas did not respond. His eyes were fixed on the devastation, seeing not what was before him now but the splendor that had once been.

"It stood there," he finally whispered, pointing with a trembling hand toward a space amid the rubble. "The Holy House... it was so small, really. Simple stones brought from Nazareth, they said. Inside was the statue of Our Lady..."

Nicholas climbed down from the wagon and stood awkwardly beside his grandfather, unsure how to respond to this display of raw emotion from a man who had always seemed unshakable.

"They burned her statue," Thomas continued, his voice hollow. "Henry's men built a great fire and threw her into it, along with statues from a hundred other shrines. They took the gold and silver, but the burning of Our Lady, that was not for profit. That was to break our hearts."

The wind gusted across the ruins, carrying the scent of distant rain. Nicholas helped Thomas to his feet, supporting him with a strength he hadn't known he possessed.

"We should make camp before nightfall," Nicholas said gently. "Where would you have us set up?"

Thomas wiped his face with the back of his hand, regaining some of his composure. "There," he said, pointing to a spot to the left side of the ruined church. "That's where it stood. The Holy House."

They made camp as the light faded, building a small fire using dead branches from the nearby woods. Thomas moved silently, mechanically, as if the sight of Walsingham's destruction had drained something vital from him. They ate a simple meal of bread and cheese, sharing a wineskin that Thomas had purchased in the last village.

"I don't understand," Nicholas finally said as they sat before the flames. "You knew it would be like this. You knew it was destroyed. Why bring me to see ruins?"

Thomas looked up, his eyes reflecting the firelight. "Because sometimes, Nicholas, what remains is as important as what was lost." He gestured around them. "They tore down the walls, but they couldn't tear down the prayers uttered here, or the faith of those who journeyed here, or the miracles that happened within these stones."

"Miracles," Nicholas repeated, unable to keep the skepticism from his voice. "Like the one you claim happened to you and Grandmother?"

"I don't claim it," Thomas said quietly. "I know it. Just as I know your mother's soul rests with God, despite the cruelty of her being taken from us too soon." He reached across to grip Nicholas's arm.

"Faith isn't certainty, my boy. It's trust despite uncertainty. It's building something that might outlast you, even if you never see it completed."

Nicholas stared into the fire, thinking of the priest hole in Dawson's house, of Margaret Clitherow's hearth with its hidden compartment, of the makeshift altar where Father William had celebrated Mass. Small acts of defiance against destruction. Preservation in the face of loss.

"Get some sleep," Thomas said finally. "Dawn comes early, and we should be away from here before too many locals notice us."

Nicholas nodded, rolling himself in his blanket near the fire. The ground was hard beneath him, but exhaustion from their journey soon dragged him toward sleep. His last conscious thought was of his mother's face—how it had looked in health, smiling as she placed his dinner on the table.

He dreamed of standing in a small stone building. Sunlight streamed through a single window, illuminating a statue on a simple pedestal. Unlike the ruins outside, everything here was whole, untouched by time or destruction. The air smelled of incense and candle wax, familiar from his childhood yet somehow more intense, more real than any church he'd ever entered.

A woman stood beside the statue, her back to him. For a heart-stopping moment, Nicholas thought it was his mother—the shape of her shoulders, the way she held her head, the dark hair falling down her back.

"Mother?" he whispered.

She turned, and Nicholas saw it was not his mother—yet there was something in her face that reminded him of her. The woman was younger, her features more delicate, yet there was a strength in her gaze that made Nicholas want to kneel.

"Your hands," she said, her voice like water over stones, "they were given to you for a purpose, Nicholas Owen."

He looked down at his hands—calloused, stained with wood oil and ink from his sketches—craftsman's hands like his father's, like his grandfather's.

"I don't understand," he said.

"You will build sanctuaries," she said, stepping closer. "Not of stone and wood alone, but of hope. My children need safe harbors in the storm that comes."

"Who are you?" Nicholas asked, though part of him already knew the answer.

She smiled, and the air around her seemed to shimmer with light. "You called me by one name, but I am known by many. To some, I am mother. To others, protector. To all, I am a refuge."

She reached out as if to touch his face, but before her fingers made contact, Nicholas felt himself being pulled back, away from the Holy House, away from her presence.

"Remember," her voice followed him like an echo. "Your hands. My children."

Nicholas woke with a start, the first gray light of dawn seeping into the sky. The fire had burned down to embers, and Thomas still slept nearby, his breathing deep and even. For a moment, Nicholas couldn't remember where he was—the stone walls of his dream had seemed so real, so solid compared to the broken ruins around him.

He sat up, his heart pounding. The dream was already fading, but the woman's face remained clear in his mind—not his mother's, yet somehow familiar. And her words still rang in his ears: *Your hands... they were given to you for a purpose.*

Nicholas looked down at his palms in the dim light. Craftsman's hands. Builder's hands. Hands that could create hiding places, sanctuaries, refuges.

For the first time since receiving news of his mother's death, Nicholas felt something shift within him—not the absence of grief, but the presence of something alongside it. A purpose, perhaps. Or the beginning of one.

The Lynn Way

The wagon creaked along the rutted road, heading south. They had left Walsingham at first light, Thomas eager to be away from the painful sight of the ruins. Nicholas sat beside him, quieter than usual, his mind still filled with images from his dream.

An hour into the journey Nicholas said, "Grandfather, I've been thinking about Master Dawson's priest hole."

Thomas glanced up, wiping water from his beard. "What of it?"

"The latch mechanism, it can be triggered accidentally. I think he should change it. Here, I have made a sketch."

Thomas studied the diagram, then looked up at his grandson with raised eyebrows. "You've given this considerable thought."

"I haven't been able to stop thinking about it," Nicholas admitted. "I think... I think I should fix it."

"You want to return to Dawson's estate?" Thomas asked. "It is a day's ride in the wrong direction."

Nicholas nodded firmly. "It's important. What if Father Edmund needs to hide there again, or another priest after him? What if the pursuivants return and search more thoroughly?" He traced the flawed joint in his drawing. "I know exactly how to correct it. It would take only a few hours' work."

Thomas studied his grandson's face carefully. Something had changed in the boy since Walsingham—a new intensity in his eyes, a certainty in his voice that hadn't been there before.

"This isn't just about the panel, is it?" Thomas asked softly.

Nicholas met his grandfather's gaze. "No," he said. "It's about... purpose. Using what I know to protect those who need protection." He hesitated. "You said faith isn't certainty. It's building something that might outlast you."

Thomas laid a hand on Nicholas's shoulder. "Your mother would be proud of the man you're becoming."

As the wagon turned toward Dawson's estate, Nicholas felt lighter than he had in weeks. The grief was still there—it would always be there—but alongside it now was something else: a sense of direction, of purpose, of being precisely where he was meant to be.

Oxford

"Nicholas? Where have you got to, boy?" Thomas's voice echoed up the narrow staircase of their Oxford home. "The Carsons will be here within the hour to discuss their commission!"

Six months had passed since their return from Walsingham. Autumn had given way to winter, and now the first tentative signs of spring appeared in the garden behind the workshop. Business had been steady, with several wealthy families commissioning furniture now that Thomas's son—Nicholas's father—had expanded their reputation through work on a side chapel at Christ Church.

When no answer came, Thomas sighed and climbed the stairs himself, his joints protesting more than they had before the long pilgrimage. "Nicholas?"

He checked the small bedroom first, finding it empty. The door to the adjoining storeroom stood slightly ajar, and Thomas pushed it open.

"Ah, there you are," he said, spotting his grandson's legs protruding from what appeared to be a solid wall beside the chimney breast. "Still making adjustments to your masterpiece?"

Nicholas wriggled backward, emerging from a narrow opening that had been invisible until he'd activated the hidden mechanism. His face was smudged with dust, but his eyes were bright with the satisfaction of a craftsman absorbed in his work.

"Almost finished," he said, brushing himself off. "I've been reinforcing the sliding panel that conceals the air vent. Come, let me show you the improvements."

Thomas followed him into the priest hole—the third Nicholas had constructed since their return, and by far the most sophisticated. This one, built into the upper floor of their own home, was Nicholas's pride.

"See how I've channeled the heat from the chimney?" Nicholas explained, tapping the wall where it met the fireplace. "In winter, this keeps the space bearable without creating visible smoke. And here—" he gestured to a narrow shelf along one wall, "—enough provisions for a week if necessary. Water flasks, hard bread, dried meat."

Thomas nodded, genuinely impressed. "And the waste?"

Nicholas pointed to a lidded bucket in the corner. "The compartment below has a removable panel. It can be emptied without the priest ever needing to emerge."

Thomas watched his grandson with pride and wonder. The boy he had worried over just months ago—angry at God, lost in grief, questioning everything—had transformed before his eyes. Nicholas still had quiet moments, times when sadness shadowed his face, but the aimlessness was gone. In its place was a sense of calm purpose.

"The Carsons will want something ornate for their dining room," Thomas said. "All the fashionable flourishes. Do you think you can tear yourself away from this work long enough to help with the designs?"

Nicholas smiled. "Of course. The visible work pays for the invisible, after all."

As they prepared to leave the priest hole, Thomas's eye caught something on the wall. It was a bas-relief of a small, simple building with a peaked roof and a single arched doorway. The carving made Thomas's chest tighten with recognition.

"The Holy House," he whispered.

Nicholas nodded. "As it appeared in my dream at Walsingham. I carved it from memory the day after we returned."

Thomas ran his finger over the perfect details—the stone pattern of the walls, the small window that allowed light to enter, the niche where the statue of Our Lady had once stood.

"You dreamed of it whole? As it was before the destruction?" Thomas asked, his voice thick with emotion.

"Yes," Nicholas said simply. "She showed it to me."

Thomas looked up sharply. "She?" Placing a hand on his arm, "Nicholas. Who showed you the Holy House?"

For a moment, the young man said nothing. Then, meeting his grandfather's eyes, he spoke quietly: "I thought at first it was Mother. But it wasn't. It was..." He hesitated. "You'll think me mad or arrogant."

"I will not," Thomas assured him.

"It was Our Lady herself," Nicholas said. "Our Lady. She told me my hands were given to me for a purpose—to build sanctuaries. Not just of wood and stone, but of hope." He gestured to the now-invisible priest hole. "This is what I was meant to do, Grandfather. This is how I serve both God and those who keep the faith."

Thomas felt tears prick his eyes. More than forty years ago, in that same Holy House, he had experienced something similar—a voice, a presence that had changed the course of his life. He had never told anyone but his wife the full truth of what happened there, fearing he would not be believed.

"I believe you," he said simply. "And I thank God every day for guiding us to Walsingham. Even in ruins, that holy place continues its work."

Nicholas nodded, emotion making speech difficult. "I still miss her," he finally managed. "Mother, I mean. Every day. But now..."

"Now the pain has purpose," Thomas finished for him. "As does your gift."

They stood in silence for a moment, the old man and the young, united by faith, by craft, by blood, and by the shared knowledge of what it meant to be touched by something beyond understanding.

"Come," Thomas said finally. "We have visible work to do. The other kind will always be waiting for your hands when the time is right."

As they descended the stairs together, Nicholas cast one last glance at the wall that concealed his creation—a sanctuary within their home, a small defiance against those who would destroy what they held sacred. In his mind, he could still see the woman's face from his dream, still hear her words.

My children need safe harbors in the storm that comes.

His hands, he had decided, would be those harbors. For as long as they were needed.

PILGRIM IN NAME ONLY

Laura Ruberto

I am only writing in this d*mn journal because my mom insisted I bring it with me. Even though of course I use my phone to write notes. She said, "You're going to need to record your trip experiences every day. What if your battery dies?" You guessed it. Dead battery. You were right, Mom. This is my first handwritten "entry"—is that what you call it?—and I want to get everything down.

I keep hearing noises, but you get used to it. Anyway, I'm too tired to take my pack off. I keep the diary in a side pocket, sealed in a plastic bag. Mom insisted so it wouldn't get wet. But don't think I'm a mama's boy. I am not. I guess you could say that I don't have the most common sense by nature though, and she knows that. Another thing I don't have is a direction in life, but I was going to change all that.

Wait. Let me back up.

My name is Giuseppino Antonio Blazic, but everyone calls me Pino. I was pushing for a cool nickname like Blaze (after our last name) as a kid, but here I am. Stupid Pino. "Peanut." "Pee-ew." "Pee-head." "Pinch the Pino." "Punch the Pino." And worse. I've heard it all. And now I'm wasting paper. Like I said, stupid.

I am on a three-month pilgrimage called the Via Francigena. Fancy name. Just means the French Way. But it's not mainly in France. And

I'm not even a pilgrim. My favorite uncle, Dino, challenged me to do it. He offered me his 1966 Alfa Romeo Spider if I finished the entire thing from Canterbury, England to Rome. You should see this car! A Series 1 Duetto. "Boattail" design. Classic grill. And it runs "like a top" as my uncle says. That's why I'm here.

Uncle Dino is cool, but also kinda Jesus-y. Ever since I was little it was Dino and Pino. Corny, yeah, but we just clicked. How many walks we took in Bosco Park with my German Shepherd dog Jakey! (I miss that good boy, but he couldn't come with me.) One summer, Uncle Dino taught me how to drive in a week in his old, camouflaged Army jeep. We used his church's giant parking lot to practice. I popped the clutch a million times, but he didn't get mad.

He's always been there for me, interested in whatever I'm doing (not much!) and trying to keep me on what he calls "the straight and narrow." We were talking about MY FUTURE, and I told him I planned to take a gap year after college. Time off. He laughed, soft-like. He's one of those people that can do that without making you feel like a total idiot. But I knew he didn't approve.

"Time off from what?"

I told him I was tired of studying and how most of my friends were doing a gap. I wanted to go to India with two of my buds—do the spiritual exploration thing over there. I thought Uncle Dino would like the religion part at least. But he didn't. He asked me to wait on my plan till he talked to me again.

A few days later he sprung it on me. He had had to check with my parents and get the details together for HIS plan. Always has his sh*t together. That's Uncle Dino. He's not really MY uncle; he's my mom's uncle. But it's weird to call someone Great Uncle. Anyway, he's from the old country. Sicily. My Great Aunt Maria passed, so it's always been "just" Uncle Dino. Wisest and toughest guy you ever want to meet. He was a wrestling coach at the high school where he taught. The team—and their parents!—practically worshipped the guy. Undefeated for years. My mom says the whole gym would be packed with the town cheering, bleachers rocking, like the pros or something. I can't relate, but I've seen pics. They look tough and happy. Went on to be "solid citizens" as he likes to say.

Well, the big thing Uncle Dino did back then was "build men of character." That's what he'll be remembered for. He's got a gift. That's the wise part of him. (The tough part was from his Army service.) He has the best advice, and he never met a problem he couldn't work through. Or as he says, pray and hope through. Dino helps people quietly, too. (Very quiet here now.) Notices what they need and tries to give it to them or help them find a way.

What he says is usually important though he doesn't talk a lot. Except when he's making a joke. Uncle Dino has a gift for telling book-length jokes. I get suckered into them all the time, thinking it's a true story when he busts out with some crazy punchline. He says he learned everything important from the "three Ms": his mom, the military and his Maria. But mostly from his faith.

That's where he and I are different. I did all the required religious stuff in our Church, but it wasn't for me. Just some rites of passage I call them. It's not that I didn't want to get something out of it (is this even what you're supposed to want?), I just never did. What's the point of it all, then?

And I'm nothing like his wrestlers either. First of all, I'm on the small side. Uncle Dino says you don't have to be big and strong to wrestle, it's about body mechanics and brains. My school didn't even have that sport, so, whatever. They were happy if more than two kids joined the bowling team. Second, I don't have that dumb "perseverance" he's always going on about. If something's that hard, I figure I don't need it or don't want it bad enough. Third, I guess I'm kinda lazy, and that does bother me sometimes, but I did okay in school. Got by. Picked an easy major. Leisure Management. Lotsa girls in it, and you got to intern at resorts and stuff. See what I mean? I'm not into the rugged stuff. Or the brainy stuff. Or the faith stuff. I'm just doing my bit. Trying to get to the "next step" and let things play out. So far, I'm doing pretty well, I'd say. I made it through college, and now I'm ready to explore the world. My parents don't agree with my outlook. They say I "lack ambition" and that you get out of life what you put in. It's true I'm not trying very hard. Like I said, what's the point?

But I am off topic… I wanted to write how I came to be on this pilgrimage thing. I've never written this much before, but I want to get some of it down. I wish I knew cursive writing. In school we didn't learn it. Mom always said it's a lot faster way to write.

It's completely silent right now. Eerie. Focus, Pino, focus. Let's see, Uncle Dino came up with this plan—or, as he called it, a "Modest Proposal." If I did the entire VF he would give me the Alfa. I was in. That car is sweet. And he must REALLY think this was a good thing to do even though I didn't know what REALLY was involved. I never even heard of the VF. Now I know it's a hike some crazy archbishop dude went on. Wrote down all the places he stopped. Or his assistant did. Something like that. About 1,000 years ago. It wasn't as exciting-sounding as India, but as Uncle Dino said, India would still be there when I got back.

He wrote up this paper with the conditions. Made it all formal. Which was actually cool. I even had to sign it. Well, I can't do an actual signature like I said about the cursive writing thing, but I wrote my name on the line. He did, too. Bernardino Alessandro Calogero. All big and bold, like John freaking Hancock!

I memorized the list of conditions.

- Solo Journey (for self-reliance, he says, I can make friends along the trail, just not partner up)
- No Mechanized Transport (unless I'm seriously bleeding or break a bone)
- Daily New Testament Reading (a chapter a day, easy)

- Sunday Mass Attendance (this is hard because you have to communicate to find the Mass times at these ancient churches)
- Visit Churches Along the Way for 10 Minutes (this one surprised me because sitting there is a cakewalk but it IS nice for the coolness and stillness after the trail, and the churches are super old and pretty cool-looking inside)
- Read the Classics (I've got a Kindle with Divine Comedy, Aeneid, Confessions, Canterbury Tales, and some other junk. Who can't read "20 minutes" a day?)
- Try Local Foods (I'm not adventurous with food, but it's not bad. Just a few mess-ups—orders that were gross—you try eating slimy eggplant!)
- No Modern Navigation Tools (hard, but the more you do it, not that bad; they have some signs along the route anyway)
- Minimal Budget (he gave me a stipend that I can make work most of the time; I have slept outside here and there)
- Keep a Daily Journal (and then weekly summary on postcard to Uncle Dino, annoying but doable)
- No Social Media (joke's on him cuz I'm not that into it in the first place)
- Learn Basic Phrases (in French and Italian)
- Acts of Kindness (one per week and document)
- Pilgrim's Credential (they have this pilgrim passport, and you get ink stamps at churches and hostels along the way—I have to make sure I prove I've been to places)
- Final Reflection at Saint Peter's (write something about the whole experience and send to Uncle Dino, I'm trying to do this one now if I can)

Was it a cr*p load of conditions? Yeah, of course. But that car! I went for it. Even with all the churchy parts. We both know you can't make someone believe in God and religion, so I think I got the better end of the deal. Free trip, some budgeting, some exercise, stop in a church here and there, a little reading and writing—not that bad. Like I said, I'm not much of a "socials" guy, so that's not terrible. Texting and gaming, sure. But three months without it isn't the end of the world. Worth it for the car.

Keep writing, Pino. Get it all down.

OK. I started in the UK. Got the Channel Tunnel to France. Then walked 500 miles. Some of the paths were relentless, but had super views from high heights. Between Folkestone and Dover was rough for me. The slippery loose stones and steep climbs and drops (some were 600 feet!) on North Downs Way gave me blisters so bad I couldn't go on. I stopped before Dover to lance them—a nice volunteer lady showed me how at the last hostel. Totally gruesome. Then you put a certain super special bandage ($$$) on them which actually worked. I couldn't believe the pain. Every step before and even after I stopped was agony. But then you get to see the famous White Cliffs... Focus, Pino. Keep writing.

You have to keep telling yourself, only nine more kilometers or whatever or just make it to the next waymarker. Remind yourself blisters are like battle scars. It's a bit of a head game. I got the hang of it after the first couple of weeks. Felt so cringe limping, but I wasn't the only one. Wish I coulda been like those mountain goats jumping around the Jura Mountain cliffs. I'm an ace at blister care now.

Oh yeah, I wanted to write about nature stuff. Of course there's the vistas. Lac de Joux will be in my heart forever. I didn't know that color existed. Like a swimming pool. Seriously. And the constant music of songbirds. (And distant church bells. Never thought I'd say that! Focus, Pino!)

Yeah, and the kestrels hunting. They go "ki-ki" when they're flying, so I always look up when I hear that. Once was over the vineyards near Reims maybe. I forget. Anyway, impressive to watch. That kind of thing can get you re-energized. I sat there mesmerized for like

10 minutes when it was eyeing then swooping down for the prey. It's a dog-eat-dog world after all.

One time I came upon a wild boar. Near Langres. Champagne region. That place I'll always remember. I was walking and there it was under a tree right by the path. Huge. Weighed 250 easy. Twice me. It eyed me and then started snorting and stamping. A lot. I froze. Next thing I hear a guy saying, "SLOWLY turn your head back toward the path. Keep walking SLOWLY. Do not run." I did what he said. So did he. Lucky for me it was a French dude who spoke English. Turns out it was a mother boar with babies behind that tree, getting in protective mode. They say to just try and pass them, but I don't know what I would've done if Pierre hadn't helped me. You need to be on your game when you're going solo.

Oh, yeah, seeing a WOLF the other day at dusk was freaky as h*ll! That time I was far enough away. Who knew they were in the Alps? I try to make a little noise now, so I don't startle any animals. There's no noise walking on snow. Want to give them time to hide. It's weird, we always say we're at the top of the food chain but not out here. Keep to the story, Pino.

So now it's been a month and a half since I started. Well, I didn't leave till August because I screwed up on the hours for an internship and needed to do another one in the summer or no BA for Pino. Not cool because that meant doing the Switzerland part of this thing during snow season. Yeah, it snows as early as October. You need snowshoes. Emergency equipment. You have to have it together. You have to have a plan. So cold. Takes some cash and work. Pilgrims do it on purpose, any time of year. They even stay at some mountain monastery with a bunch of volunteers and priests.

The true believers are into all of this. Pino is not. Ha. P. I. N. O. Pilgrim In Name Only. What a joke. I'm not part of whatever the others are experiencing. I'm just walking and doing all "the conditions" for the prize. Alone. What did I get myself into?

I'm only halfway through the VF. In the Alps. I'm under a bit of rock outcrop waiting out a massive snowfall. And—I'm lost. Just when I was thinking, hey, I can use my stupid degree for something here. Like work at a place on the trail and help hikers. And maybe meet a nice girl. Oh man. I could... D*mn, I dropped the pencil in the snow again. It's hard to hold it.

They said a storm could come up at any moment, but it was 100% clear when I set out. Cell battery ran out. Last thing I did was activate an emergency locator beacon before my phone died, but who knows if it worked. Fire's out now. Nothing to burn. So tired. Last food was yesterday. Or the night before? My Apple Watch stopped. I'm hoping the snow will make my cave more insulated but I'm already frozen.

I wish my Jakey was here. Sleeps at the end of my bed every night. Warms my feet. Bet he's wondering where I am now. Good buddy. Looks like he's smiling all the time. Had him since I was 10. Old, but always ready for a walk around the neighborhood.

We have met girls on those neighborhood walks. (They only wanted to pet Jake, but still.) What if I did meet a special one and get married? I haven't even been on a real date. Jemma asked me to that Sadie Hawkins dance junior year. That doesn't count though since her dad was driving. I don't know if it should be now. I'm scared of it really. But pumped too. I need someone who can help me. I want to be a better person. It's hard. You need someone to believe in you. I would believe in her, too. I could see that happening. But who would want me now?

Want. What I want. Come on, Pino! What I want to say is I turned a corner—though I hated all the discipline, blisters, acts of kindness (and they WERE acts at the beginning) and reading. At first. All of it. I think I was starting to get the lessons Uncle Dino wanted me to learn. It was coming together and now I blew it. All I want now is to survive. It's been a LONG time since my last scrap of bread. Feeling desperate, like that guy from the start of the trip. Someone stole his wallet. No moola for food or water. I got him a meal at the next café.

You never know when it might be you. Sergio from Spain, he was. Easy to remember that one.

That do-gooder attitude didn't help me now, though. I gave my nice windbreaker to a girl who was shivering one night at the hostel. (Told you I'm small.) She hadn't prepared at all and just started hiking because a guy she liked was doing it. She had a big floppy hat.

Oh yeah. A hat. I mean baseball cap. Had AMU on it. Someone lost it. Funny. It was in the weeds when I went to take a leak. I decided to leave it on a bench outside the next church. Some chick Sophie saw me. Says in English, "Is that your hat?" It was her friend's hat from Ave Maria U. Cool. She was happy. I was happy, too. Maybe I'll see them again, but not now. It's never gonna happen... Come on, Pino. Don't go there. You sound like that couple from Canada.

Those two. Nightmare. Constantly arguing. Then screaming at each other. Kept pace with me. Couldn't shake them. I have to admit, they were fit. At the rest stop we filled our water bottles. She was crying. He went to touch her. She flinches. What the h*ll? Then he starts telling me their 20-year-old daughter just died of the big C. The whole story comes out. Sh*t! I don't want to hear it, man. But I stay. Seems like telling a stranger helps them. I get this idea. Ask them to tell me some stories about her. They do. Sebastian and Mags. Daughter Isabel. Good people.

Another rest area near Canterbury. Litter everywhere. Complained the whole time I picked it up. Muttering to myself. At least the next people found it nice. Nice. People. Little boy gave me a water bottle from the bottom of his kid brother's stroller. How did he know I had left mine at the hostel and was thirsty? Some people, not nice. Waiting for the ferry to Calais. Old geezer yelling at me. I went in front of him in line. Not on purpose. It wasn't clear where the dumb line was. I decided not to get ticked. Just nodded to him. That shut him down. If everyone would take a pause sometimes, the world would be better.

Sounds like Uncle Dino. Ha. Nodded. Nodding off. Important... Stay awake. As messed up as I am, I'm different now. I want to live. Make a plan. Pino, the man with the plan. Ha ha.

Eyes all blurry. Coldest cold. Hard to write. I need to. Wait. Is that? Oh. Jakey!

I'm back. I decided to do one more note. The story has an ending. Would you believe I'm in that hospice monastery place for pilgrims at Great Saint Bernard Pass? Yep. They are taking great care of me. Observing me for a week after my ordeal. I'm actually gaining weight. One of the monks invited me to Mass. I'm still thinking about it.

I was frozen and delirious in that cave, writing about everything and nothing, sure I'd never see the sun again. That's right before I passed out. I wrote "Jakey" because a dog face was poking its head over the top layer of snow at the cave entrance. It wasn't Jakey of course, but I was found. It was a Saint Bernard called Matteo (means hope—for real!). They have these rescue dogs here, and my beacon thingy worked! They told me that Matteo's bark brought the rescue team.

I have had time to reflect (as Uncle Dino says). I know I'm not the same kid who started the Via Francigena. It doesn't matter that it was bribery that got me out here, does it? I told Dino on the phone I'm thinking of staying over here and getting work at a resort or hostel. For real. He agrees with my idea and wants us to go right to Sicily! He wants to introduce me to family (of course) and ALSO to some friends who happen to have a small hotel. If anyone has "connections," it's Uncle Dino. I looked up the area. (That's me taking initiative. Ha!) Guess what—it's near a pilgrim camino that has been revived. Turns out Sicily has tons of caminos crisscrossing the island and zero snow-storms that I know of.

Anyway, I can't wait to see him next week and get one of his bear hugs. I'll bear hug him right back—told you I'm stronger now. We'll leave for Sicily as soon as I get the okay from the docs. Meantime,

I'm taking notes on how they provide hospitality for travelers here at the monastery. They've been doing it for 900 years. There's a lot I can learn. Like Dino says, everything happens for a reason.

Maybe I should ask him about that...

A VERY JURASSIC PILGRIMAGE

Corinna Turner

I measure the distance to the shrine on the DashConsole. The sun is low, but...

"We're so close! We'll be there tonight!"

Uncle Ted leans to put a work-roughened fingertip on the screen.

"As the eagle flies, Kateri. But look at the terrain." A touch of his fingers zooms in.

"So many crags." My heart sinks. "Can't we get through?"

"Not in a HabVi. We gotta go around." His finger traces the route. "Fifteen miles. Rough going. We'll have to finish the journey in the morning."

I sit back with a sigh. A Habitat Vehicle is great off-road—huge ground clearance, massive wheels, tilting rear axles, bristling with winches for self-recovery. But we can't go everywhere. The sooner we get there, the sooner we—

"Oh, not now!" Dad's angry mutter draws my gaze to the front windshield.

A she-rex and her juvenile daughter stand in our way. Even the juvenile is thirty feet long with seven-inch teeth. They eye the large vehicle as though unsure whether the humans inside are edible or dangerous.

Since we're Hunters, not city-folk...both.

I stay motionless, aware of Uncle Ted equally unmoving beside me.

Dad lays on the horn and flicks on the strobe light on the observation turret. Trying to spook them?

"Dad!" Why don't he just stay still and wait for them to go?

They flinch back slightly, but continue staring, eyes focusing on the windshield. They can see Dad moving.

"Go on, *git*!" Dad slams his fist into the steering wheel, yelling as though they can understand him. "Clear off or I'm gonna get the rex gun and shoot you both, so help me God!"

"*Dad!*"

Uncle Ted catches my arm in a firm but gentle grip, and shakes his head. A slight frown wrinkles his tanned forehead. Yeah, Dad's in a mood to be left alone. But facing off with T. rex is dangerous! Our HabVi's armor is only rated up to allosaurs, nothing larger.

Dad inches toward them, revving and flashing the lights and honking. With one last suspicious look at us, they leave.

The tension in my ribcage eases as I watch them go. The mother pads along, strong and healthy, her daughter following close at her heels. Confident. Happy. Another kind of tension tightens my chest, hurting worse than the first.

Dad drives on, a thundercloud on his brow. He didn't really wanna come. But it don't matter. Once we get to the shrine and pray, Saint Desmond will heal Mom, I know he will. Mom loves 'saurs, just like Saint Des, who lived alone and unprotected among them for so long. If only Dad had agreed to come sooner. But I guess it don't make no difference to God and Saint Des how sick she is, they can heal her just the same.

We're already moving into craggy ground. Darkness spreads from the outcrops around us.

"Gonna have to stop soon," Uncle Ted grunts eventually, when Dad still shows no sign of doing so.

Dad don't reply, but when we reach a safe spot he finally lets us roll to a halt. He applies the handbrake and lowers the stabilizers for the night.

"Should I make some food?" I say hesitantly.

"I don't want nothing," Dad snaps. He goes on sitting at the wheel, not moving. Finally, he thumps it again with his fist and shoots me an angry glare. "Why you wanna be out here, instead of with your mother and your little sibs, at a time like this—" He breaks off, shakes his head, then rises and ducks through into the living area.

I sit still, not looking at Uncle Ted, because my eyes are full of tears and my throat feels so tight. I guess we're safe enough and I could cry, but nothing feels safe right now. With Mom lying there on her—

Uncle Ted puts his arm around me and gives me a quick squeeze. "Chin up, Kateri. Your mom wanted you to come. Just remember that."

I want a proper hug, but I make myself sit up straight. Mom keeps telling me how I'm gonna be the mother of the family soon. Even though I'm only fifteen and ain't even that smart.

But I don't need to worry about that. Because... "Saint Des can heal her. I know it."

His face falls. "Oh, Kateri. Of course he *could*, but that kinda thing ain't the norm, cub. We'd have to be real lucky to be blessed that way."

"Mom believes it."

"Your Mom believes that *you* need to come here, cub. As for herself—she's made her peace with it, even if you and your dad ain't yet."

Am I the *only* one here who understands that we're on a mission to save Mom?

I get up and follow Dad into the living area, Uncle Ted behind me. Dad's bent over the main console, reading a message, so I head toward the kitchen area. I ain't very hungry neither, but we gotta keep our strength up so we can make a quick start in the morning, get to the shrine as soon as possible.

Dad swears—actually swears. He straightens, grabs the picture of Saint Desmond the Hermit from over the console, rips it from the wall, crumples it, and throws it to the floor.

"Dad!" I lunge and pick it up. I try to straighten out the creases, but it's never gonna look the same. This is Mom's favorite!

But Dad just stares at Uncle Ted, his face all pale and strained-looking.

"What's up?" Uncle Ted asks warily.

"She's taken a real turn for the worse. I *knew* this were a mistake. First thing tomorrow, we head home."

"What?" My fists clench on the picture, crumpling it again. "But we're *so* close! Just a couple of hours, and she can be healed! We can't go back now!"

"We can and we will. I've had enough of this nonsense. She shouldn't have encouraged you! Now it'll be worse for you than if we hadn't come at all, but I'll be dead and devoured if I'm gonna let her die without us by her side! We go back at first light! If you're gonna pray for something, pray we get there in time!"

He reaches the cab bedroom in two long strides and disappears inside. The door slides closed and the lock clicks.

"Uncle Ted, we can't!" I protest.

But he just looks at me sadly and shakes his head. Okay, he's been Dad's assistant since before time began, and he has full camp rights for himself and his family at the Chiwatenhwa camp, and he might as well *be* blood family. But he ain't. And he has no say over where this vehicle goes.

So at dawn, it'll head home.

And Mom will die.

Once Uncle Ted has nibbled at a hard biscuit, sipped a cup of Joe, and turned in, I'm left sitting alone at the fold-down table. I stare at the biscuits, but can't make myself eat. Then I call up the map on the main console and stare at that instead.

We're so close. We could *walk* there and back before dawn, taking the direct route, we're so darn close!

Or...

I could?

I mean...it ain't like Saint Des would let me get eaten when I'm on my way to see him, right?

The hatch through the rear door opens very quietly. I slip through, legs first, and lower myself to the ground. Lift my rifle through very carefully, so it don't clang. Close the hatch silently. Then lock it again so nothing can get in.

I leave my headlight off as I tip-toe away from the 'Vi. Dad or Uncle Ted might be looking out. The tiny bit of moon ain't enough. I grope my way along, stubbing my toes on rocks and trying to make sure my rifle don't knock against nothing.

Finally, the 'Vi is out of sight. I turn on my red headlight. That's better. And the red light will show up less than white. Not that any predators will bother me. Saint Des will make sure of that.

Right, Saint Des?

My heart still pounds real hard as I move further and further from the safety of the 'Vi. I check the mapPad in my hand. I gotta be there and back by dawn. Dad didn't tell me I *couldn't* go there, after all. He just said we were leaving at dawn. S'long as I'm back by then, I ain't disobeyed him, not really.

I'll have broken every other safety rule in the book, but I won't have *disobeyed* him. Exactly.

My stomach churns as I walk, all the same. I ignore the feeling. Mom's life is at stake. If I don't do this...we won't have her around no more. My chest hurts, just thinking about it.

How can we manage without her? I'm fairly bright for a 'happy child'—the polite term among hunters—but I *ain't* smart. Jean can already do more math than me and he's only eight. How can I fill Mom's boots?

My chest is tight and panicky. I *need* Mom. *We* need Mom! Dad's been so grumpy since she got sick. What if he stays that way forever?

No, if I can get to the shrine and pray, Saint Des will ask God to make her better. And everything will be okay.

I check the mapPad. I can't see that far ahead, but it's an easy route. Mostly game trails. That outcrop should be this one…yes, I still know where I am.

I scramble up what I hope is a shortcut. Except for a water bottle slung over one shoulder and my semi-automatic hunting rifle over the other, and the packet of hardtack in my pocket, I ain't got nothing to weigh me down. If I get there by about one in the morning to pray, I can make it back by dawn. I can.

My breath creates a haze in the red light as I pant harder and harder. The temperature is dropping. Despite all the exercise, I zip my coat all the way up to the neck. Shoulda checked the weather. Is it gonna snow?

I did put on my snow pants and good parka, thank Saint Des. I won't die of cold. Not unless I sit down in one spot.

I slide down a scree slope and get back onto an easier game trail. Let's hope nothing's using it. Nothing bigger and meaner than me, anyways. My rifle makes a reassuring weight across my back.

A rifle's only any use if you see the danger coming.

Saint Des, protect me.

Shivering, I hurry on. According to the mapPad, I ain't halfway there yet. *Great.*

I round a large boulder and something moves a few feet away. I freeze. Whatever it is must be holding still too. I ease my rifle around and into position. I slip my finger inside the trigger guard.

What is it?

I gotta get past. So I inch along the path, keeping my rifle pointed toward the spot.

What *is* that? Something pale shows in the red light. Practically pure white. And...feathered? A snowy owl? Is it hurt?

I move closer, trying to see. Too big for an owl. It's almost velociraptor-sized, as big as a large dog with plenty more tail.

It jerks away from the light, pressing against the boulder I just walked around.

Trying to hide.

"It's okay. I ain't gonna hurt you."

It don't look like nothing I recognize. I crouch and shuffle closer.

"Hey, little fella. What are you?"

It turns around for a moment, and I catch a look at its bare leathery face. I glance at its feet. Yep, huge killing claws on each one, looking out of scale with the rest of the critter. I steady the rifle, but... Yeah, downy feathers cover it. It's a nestling.

"You look like a Dakotaraptor, but you're the wrong color. You should be brown with a colored ruff. Russet brown or chocolate brown or amber brown or...well, there are so many beautiful Dakota shades. But you're...*white*. All over."

Hang on... quickly, I look all around me. This critter looks only just old enough to toddle after its mother. Am I near a nesting ground?

Cold sweat breaks out all over me. No, Saint Des has my back. I'm on my way to his special place. Besides...

I stare at the frightened chick. It's shivering hard. I reach out a hand towards it, and it jerks back, only to collapse on its tummy. Gripping its muzzle firmly, I slide a finger into the corner of its mouth, where there ain't no teeth. It's cold inside. Not good.

"You're all alone, ain't you?"

Poor thing. It'll die for sure.

It pulls free with a nervous *cheep.* "It's okay, little fella." I imagine the sounds a raptor-mom would make to soothe it, and try to imitate them. It stops shrinking away and stares at me more hopefully. "Hey, it's okay." I stroke its back, hoping it feels like a mother nuzzling it. "It's okay, Snowy. I'll take care of you."

I pull out a biscuit, bite off a chunk, and chew it up. Then spit it into my hand and try to feed it to the chick. Carefully. Its head is already larger than a velociraptor's. It could bite me quite badly. It…no, he…is confused to start with. Used to partially digested meat, not soggy hardtack. But he gets the idea and gobbles the biscuit goo eagerly. Then he nuzzles at my hand for more, shivering and pressing against me. I chew and feed for a while, but I'm getting colder and colder sitting here, and so is he.

"Okay, you seem to be friendly. Come here, then." I unzip my coat, gather him to my chest, and zip it up around him. With the bottom fastened tightly, it holds him up okay. He wriggles slightly, then settles against me. Exhausted? Or enjoying the warmth?

Both?

His chilly body sucks the heat from me. How long has he been out here? I need to get him some help.

I check my mapPad carefully. I'm still slightly closer to the 'Vi than to the shrine. But it's almost all downhill to the shrine, and uphill to the 'Vi. It will be quicker to take him to the shrine. And I sure don't wanna give up on Mom.

Besides, the mood Dad's in at the moment, would he look after a raptor chick or throw it back outside? The shrine has a raptor sanctuary. It's the perfect place for him.

I arrange my rifle as comfortably as I can, now that Snowy is in the way of my strap, and get to my feet.

"*Saint Des's toenails*, you're heavier than you look!" I gasp.

I can't slow down, though. I can't. I still have to be back at the 'Vi before dawn.

Trying to ignore the weight, I hurry on.

I'm panting. Each step is so hard. I'm so cold. I hope Snowy is okay inside my jacket. He's as warm as I can make him, anyway.

How much farther? I fumble the mapPad out and check. My heart sinks. It's still so far. Over a mile. I don't think I can keep going much longer. Snowy is *so* darn heavy. I wish he could get out and walk, but he still feels too cool, even after being in my coat all this time. I gotta keep carrying him.

I stumble on a boulder and fall. Again. My knees sting as I struggle to my feet. It's past two o'clock. How can I get back in time?

Forget "back in time," Kateri Mary Desmelda Chiwatenhwa, I tell myself. *Worry about getting there at all.*

Yeah. I'm getting real tired and real cold, and it's still real far. This ain't good. But I won't leave Snowy. His pack left him. Maybe even his mother left him. But I won't!

My legs shake under me. A loose stone sends me to the ground again.

I drag myself up. Drag myself on. Clinging to the rock walls of the ravine to keep myself upright.

It's too far. I can't go on. I can't...

A few more steps and we're at the top of the slight rise, and the path falls away, heading downhill again. And there at the bottom of the slope...

Red lights. Sudden hope catches my breath. Is that the outer fence of the shrine estate? It must be.

I stumble downhill. Adrenalin makes my legs a little stronger. Soon the fence looms above me. The red lights glow steadily on top of the posts, warning that it's live. What sort of fence is it? Wildlife only or security too? An outer fence, this far out from the main complex will just be for wildlife, right? So it should have...

I put a hand on the nearest post to steady myself so I don't fall on the wires. Then lift the flap on the control box. Yes! I grab the red switch and turn it to 'emergency off.' The steady red light on the pole changes to a violently flashing green. Green because the electricity is off. Violently flashing because...the electricity is off.

I sink down at the base of the post, hugging Snowy. I'm shivering so hard.

"We're gonna be okay," I whisper to Snowy.

I'm too tired to do anything but sit. Until a snuffling sound from behind the fence makes me glance around. My red light illuminates slightly parted lips, razor sharp teeth...

I jerk away onto hands and knees.

Three Utahraptors, the biggest species of all, stare at me from feet away. The large female stretches out her neck again, sniffing at the fence. Almost like she's...checking for power?

Saint Desmond's armpits!

I lurch to my feet, grab the power switch, and turn it back to 'live.' The light changes to amber strobe as the controller lets out a rapidly accelerating beeping, ending on a high continuous tone before the light goes back to steady red.

Hissing, the—one-eyed?—raptor recoils.

Phew! I guess most of the land inside the fence is used for the raptor sanctuary. I shoulda realized the fence might be keeping some'at in as well as out.

I sink down again, further from the live wires. Snowy shifts weakly inside my coat and settles again. I unzip it just enough to feed him more chewed-up biscuit. My eyelids are so heavy.

I should stay awake. I should. I blink and try to keep watch, turning my head this way and that to redden the night. Just gotta stay awake...

...Mom looks so thin and pale now. A tube in her arm helps with the pain. A tube under her nose helps her breathe. I hate seeing her like this. If Dad would just take me to the shrine...

But her face is so peaceful as Father Anders holds the golden Host in front of her eyes.

I stare at her face as she receives God. As she closes her eyes to pray. Trying to understand what I'm seeing. Her expression is so...so... I don't even know.

I have to get to the shrine. I have to save her...

An engine roars nearby. I lift my head. Oh no, were I asleep? Headlights move along the fence toward me. I drag myself to my feet.

Snowy weighs *so* much! Moments later, light dazzles me as a hunting truck stops a short distance away. The silhouette of a man and a rifle pop up into the domed cage-turret on the roof, providing cover. By the time I've taken several weary steps in that direction, the passenger door opens and another man gets out.

"Into the truck, you look half-frozen." He steps toward me, then jerks to a halt. "What in Saint Des's name—?" He's staring at my legs.

I look down too. Snowy's long tail dangles from the bottom of my jacket. "I found a lost chick." My jaw feels cold and numb, making me talk funny. "I were trying to get him to the shrine, but I couldn't walk no farther. He's real heavy."

The man puffs out a breath, making a plume of mist. He shakes his head, then guides me to the back door of the truck.

"Come on, in you go, chick and all." He climbs in after me. "I'm Brother Bill, by the way." The other guy takes his head and shoulders from the turret and sits back in the driver's seat, giving me a big smile as he settles his rifle by the parking brake. "And this here is Father Nathan."

"I'm K-Kateri." My teeth are chattering so hard. Brother Bill looks of Northern European ancestry, like Mom. Father Nathan looks more Hispanic, mebbe some Native American too. Not sure what. Dad's Huron blood is rare. Both clearly Hunters. They wear identical jeans and brown tunics, with brown parkas thrown on top. "Are you Saint Desmond's monks?"

"Order of Saint Desmond, yes. Although technically brothers, not monks," says Father Nathan.

"Never mind that now, what is it you found out there?" asks Brother Bill. "That's one weird tail."

I unzip my coat to show Snowy, sleeping peacefully against my chest. They both jerk back slightly.

"Sheesh! Dakotaraptor!"

"Albino," says Father Nathan, leaning forward again for a closer look.

Now he says it, I recognize the word. "Is that why he's all white?"

"Yeah," says Brother Bill. "What a beauty. He's too big to be that close to you, though."

"Oh, don't take him away! He's so cold already."

"Hmm." Brother Bill fishes around behind the seat for a moment, emerging with a handful of cable ties. Then he reaches out and lifts Snowy into his lap, claws safely outwards. He slips a cable tie around Snowy's mouth as a makeshift muzzle. A pair of work gloves go onto Snowy's killing claws and another pair onto his wing claws, also secured with cable ties. "Okay," he says, "now you can keep him warm by cuddling him." Snowy makes a few smothered *peeps* of protest as Brother Bill slides him back across the seat to me.

"It's okay." I stroke him gently. "It's okay, we're going somewhere warm, okay?"

"So, cub," says Brother Bill, as Father Nathan pulls away. "What are you doing out here alone, and in the middle of the night, at that?"

And a cub like you, his worried eyes add. *With an extra chromosome?* But I guess he's too polite to say that out loud.

Something tickles my nose. I open my eyes. Feathers. Snowy's feathers. I'm lying in the straw beside him in the Raptor Sanctuary's nursery unit, and he's sleeping. He now sports proper claw-caps on all four big claws, and a far more comfortable mesh nursing muzzle. It's got a hole for a bottle of liquidized meat, like the one I fed him after we arrived.

"Where is she?" Dad's voice echoes from the corridor. "You sure she's okay?"

Something heavy sinks in my stomach. What *time* is it? The light on the straw in front of me is…sunlight. Oh no!

"Here we are." Father Nathan's voice. I lie very still. Will he be *really* angry?

"*What the—*"

"Yeah, she picked that not-so-little one up along the way. Carried it for miles. Insisted on looking after it when we got here, before eating anything herself."

Dad snorts. "Sounds like Kateri. She'd mother a mad dog, she's so good with little 'uns. And she's smart. I know you wouldn't think it to look at her, but she is. *Wilderness* smart. Not book smart. I knew she could get herself here, just fine—I were only afraid of some'at eating her."

He don't *sound* angry. But he's always angry these days. I carry on pretending to be asleep.

Smart. Dad thinks I'm smart. And a good mother. Even though I've already warmed up thoroughly, that makes me feel toasty inside.

"Well, this thing's real tame," says Father Nathan. "Gonna have a nice life here at the sanctuary as our new mascot, I reckon. Pack probably abandoned it because it looks different, poor critter."

"Thank God for that," says Dad. *Huh?* His voice shakes oddly as he adds, "Just think if they'd followed it."

A grunt of agreement from Father Nathan.

"Did she..." Dad pauses, clears his throat. "Did she tell you why she came?"

"Yeah."

I sit up with a gasp. *Oh no!* I told them in the truck, but then we got to the complex and I were so busy making sure Snowy were okay and then I fell asleep and...

"Dad!" I struggle to my feet. *Ouch.* All my muscles hurt, everywhere. "Dad, please, please, please can I go to the shrine and pray, *real quick,* before we go? *Please?*"

Dad's arms go around me, and the next moment I'm crushed to his broad chest. "Kateri, you crazy, crazy girl!" he whispers. "You scared the life outta me! And you've given Ted grey hairs."

"Sorry, Dad. I just want Mom to be okay."

"So do I, sweetie. So do I. But..." Dad's voice goes hesitant. "Mebbe...mebbe it ain't up to us to say what okay means for her."

What? I pull back, staring at his face. "Are you decoying me? You saying you're okay with her...with her..."

He pulls me hard against him again. "I don't know nothing about nothing, no more," he whispers. "I just know that when I were begging Saint Des to give you back to me alive, I promised I wouldn't be mad at him or God no more. We can go to the shrine. On one condition."

"What?"

"That you ask for what's best for Mom. Not you. Not me. Not the little'uns. Mom."

Since they ain't open yet, Father Nathan unhooks a few rope barriers and lets us walk all around Saint Desmond's cave. There's the fire pit, with its metal hood and chimney to take the smoke outside. One of the few 'luxuries' he allowed himself. There's his bed, carved into the rock. Looks uncomfortable, but he didn't care because he loved living out here with God and nature so much.

Here's the alcove where he kept sick animals and 'saurs. Like his most famous friend, Beauty the Dakotaraptor. He nursed her back to health, and she loved him forever.

"That's his little oratory," Father Nathan tells us softly, indicating another side chamber. A red light tells us that Our Lord is present in the fancy golden box in the wall above a small stone altar. "And his tomb, of course."

There it is! In the rear wall of the oratory. A simple slab with just his name.

Father Nathan points to a small cross inset into the floor in the main living area. "That's where he were taken ill, or so forensics concluded. And where Beauty probably found him, before she went to fetch help."

The most famous story of all!

"And he crawled to the oratory?" I say. "And died at the foot of the altar?"

Father Nathan nods. Then points to something else. "He crawled past his radio on the way, without stopping. Our Lord were the only comfort he wanted."

I think about that. "Most people would be so scared of dying, they'd wanna talk to someone, even if no one could help them?" I say slowly. "But Saint Des loved God so much, he weren't scared at all?"

Father Nathan nods. "We're all gonna go sometime. It's how we go that matters."

It ain't Saint Des's face that fills my mind now. It's Mom's. The peace on her face as Father Anders gave her "Last Rites" a few days ago. The…joy. That's what it were. *Joy.* I couldn't figure it out.

I go to kneel at the little altar in front of God, on the very spot where the great saint died. Dad kneels beside me.

When we finally get up to leave, I shoot a look at Dad. His eyes are wet.

"Mom's like Saint Des, ain't she?" I ask him. "Not scared at all."

He pulls me close again. Breathes out shakily. "Yeah. Yeah, she is."

"And Saint Des ain't gonna heal her. Because he'd be doing it for us. Not for her."

Dad kisses my forehead. "Yeah, sweetie. We have to let her fly free. Though it took your unauthorized foot patrol to make me realize."

"Realize?"

"People gotta be true to themselves. No matter what."

I take Mom one of Snowy's white feathers, and a little chip of stone from Saint Des's cave wall. I think she understands what they are. I put them gently in her hand and she smiles, anyways.

I ask Father Anders to bring out the monstrance, so Mom can be with Him. Just like Saint Des.

In the night, a familiar-looking man comes up to the bed wearing jeans and a brown tunic, just like the Order of Saint Desmond. But I don't remember meeting him at the shrine. Or did I? He holds out a hand to Mom and she takes it. And they walk right into the monstrance and disappear in a burst of golden light.

When I lift my head from my chest, blinking, Dad's sobbing and Mom's lying too still.

Gabriel's in his crib and Jo is already in bed, so I lift Jean onto my hip and carry him out of the room just like I carried Snowy through the wilderness. I get him a snack and tuck him in for what's left of the night. When he's asleep I go back to Mom and Dad's room.

And nestle in Dad's arms. And cry. And cry. And cry.

But even though it feels like one of the sanctuary's Utahraptors has ripped my heart from my chest...I ain't afraid no more.

Mom's okay. And we're gonna be okay too.

NOT ALL WHO WANDER

Rietta Parker

The Dean at Tulane thinks I'm the guy who decapitated their statue of the Virgin Mary, and I don't know how to prove I'm innocent.

Well, it's not their statue. I guess it's the international pilgrimage office's statue. I used to vandalize all the time and have been on probation since the start of the summer semester. One more slip-up and I can "kiss graduation in August goodbye," as the dean put it. And now, the image of Mary headless is blowing up in the news, and this vandalizing I didn't do could cost me my degree from Tulane.

"Hey. Char. Charmon. Hello? Are ya here?"

I blink and focus on Maria's hand waving back and forth in front of my face. We're on our annual summer Sno-La tour: shove as much syrupy ice down your gullet as you can in a day, try not to barf, and rate them all. We've saved the usual best for last: William's Plum Street Snowballs.

"Of course I'm here. Are you blind?" I guzzle the rest of my strawberry cheesecake snowball and avoid eye contact.

Maria gives me a look and elbows me in the ribs, "I asked you a question."

"Hmm? When?"

"About 3 minutes ago." She cracks my favorite close-mouthed smile.

I don't try to force one in response. "Oh."

Her smile fades. "I asked if you heard about the Mary statue that got vandalized. It literally got decapitated."

I sigh, responding in a clipped tone, "Yeah, I heard."

Another three minutes pass in silence, and this time Maria doesn't try to snap me out of it. Instead, she pushes her melting ice around its Chinese-takeout-esque-box (one of the best things about William's), biting her lower lip. Meanwhile, I grip my plastic spoon harder than necessary, biting down on its empty bowl.

At about the five-minute mark, she can't take it anymore.

"Alright, Char. Please, make it stop. My snowball is a snow-river now."

The force of my teeth against the bowl finally causes the spoon to snap off its handle, and I get up to throw it and my empty box away. When I turn back around, Maria's head is cocked to the side. Never a good sign. I stuff my hands in my jean pockets and stare at a fat pigeon pecking at the concrete beneath us.

"Char. You-you didn't—"

"Didn't what?" I squeeze my eyes, cringing.

"You know…"

"No, I really don't."

"Oh come on, Char." My name sounds off, like she almost skirts around it.

I wish I'd kept the spoon so my hands would have something to do other than curl in on themselves. "Maria, I told you. I'm not that guy anymore." The chirpy bell on the door of the snowball place dings.

I can feel her glowering at me. "Where were you last night?"

"Can't say." I wish I could say, so I could prove myself innocent for once.

She puts down her snow-river. "You can't say? Are you kidding?"

"Nope."

She throws up her arms. "I don't believe you," and her snow-river goes waterfalling over the edge of the bench. I snap my head up, finally making eye contact with her, willing her to believe me, but all I see in her eyes is disbelief and…disgust.

I bite out in a low voice, "I don't appreciate being backed into a corner, okay, Maria?"

She shakes her head and takes her turn staring at the pigeon now basically bathing in the syrupy ice river at her feet.

I sigh. "Look, I'll see you later, okay?" Without waiting for a response, I shoo the pigeon, clean up the evidence of her snowball massacre, and leave.

If I hadn't been with Doug, the idiot, who's won the gold star achievement in life of being on the FBI's Most Wanted List, I could give my alibi. But, what do I say now? No, I didn't do it. I was with my friend, Doug, in his secret French Quarter apartment where he's successfully hidden from the FBI for the last 30-something years. Here's his address if you wanna book him! I should've never sat with Doug at Café du Monde.

It's a tradition of mine to end my meandering around the French Quarter at 3:00 a.m. every Saturday night by grabbing a table. One night I noticed Doug: a middle-aged guy with the kind of bald head that makes you sure there was never any hair on it in the first place, and a multitude of unexpected arm tattoos like flowers and Madonna. Doug noticed me noticing him:

"Hey kid, what are ya looking at?"

I looked over my shoulder and back at him. "Oh, uh I don't know. I like your tattoos?"

He stared at me for a while. I wondered if maybe I should carry a pocket knife.

"Ya sure there's not another reason?" My eyes drifted to the side. Was there another reason? No, I decided, and shook my head. He blinked, then his stone face broke into a huge smile, and I saw he was missing a couple of teeth on either side of the bottom row. I gave him an awkward smirk in return. His smile faded, and he looked around him and then up, as if he was searching for something. He shrugged to himself, "Well, wanna join me?"

I blinked. "Eh, sure? Why not." I picked up my plate of beignets and ambled over to the chair across from him, plopping down a little too aggressively, the powdered sugar littering the air.

Doug sneezed and laughed, "I'm Doug."

"I'm Charmon." I gave another awkward smile. He stared at me again. I felt squeamish and pushed my beignets aside.

"Ya don't go by that, do you?"

"No." He squinted at me, waiting. I cleared my throat. "I'm Char." Doug flashed his toothless grin again and started rapidly asking me all kinds of questions which the alcohol responded to: Where ya from, Char? What brought ya to Nola? Gotta girl? Oh, so you *want* a girl? (I grimaced.) What do ya wanna be? How long ya got at Tulane?

Around 4:00 a.m. I got up and stretched, my fingers curling into fists, powdered sugar scraping my palms. Doug was staring a lot again.

"Welp, I should probably go..."

"One more question: Why were ya here tonight?"

"I come here every Saturday night..." He bobbed his head to himself. I took his silence as my cue finally to go, and nodded goodbye to him.

The next Saturday he was there in the same spot, and I couldn't help myself: I sat with him.

Now once I'm done roaming from one cast iron balcony to the next, I prefer to slip through the decaying wooden door on Dauphine Street that leads to Doug's secret apartment, which is cool except for the whole running-from-the-FBI-cause-he-led-a-bunch-of-armed-robberies-in-his-20s thing. Doug starts making popcorn on the stove around 2:00 a.m. 'cause he knows I'm a sucker for salty snacks, and visiting him has become my new ritual. We take turns asking the other as many questions as we want. One of Doug's first turns of course focused on wanting to know more about the girl:

"So, ya aren't gonna ask Maria out?"

"No."

"Why not?"

"'Cause I'm not Catholic."

"And ya think because of this she'll say no?"

"Yes."

"But ya don't vandalize anymore?"

"That doesn't change me not being Catholic. It just means I'm not as ... impulsive ... about it as I once was."

"But there's gotta be a reason why you don't do it anymore. Is it for her?"

"No, cause again it doesn't make a difference. I'm still not Catholic."

"Then why?"

"I don't know."

"Okay."

And that was the extent of it.

When I get back from the snowball massacre, I re-read the email from the dean of Tulane asking me to come into his office tomorrow morning. I wonder if this is God's way of punishing me for the many times before now that I did vandalize. Maybe Mike and Eddie framed me. They hate me now that I don't want to help tear apart rosaries and scatter the beads across the campus chapel floor, or draw a mustache on the canvas painting of Mary holding baby Jesus in the Catholic student center. If I close my eyes, I can still see their dumb scrunched-up faces when they explained, "Mary's the one we hate the most. She's just a chick who got knocked up."

I used to justify vandalizing Mary on account of most other Christians not seeming to think she was that big of a deal. I felt I wasn't tempting fate as much as, say, defacing a crucifix. But the first time I really talked to Maria, you know, instead of asking questions that warranted a one-word response that was probably a lie, she talked about her love for Mary. It's not for Maria that I stopped vandalizing but rather maybe because of her.

"So, what's your biggest issue with Catholicism?" Maria asked.

"The whole worshiping Mary baloney. I mean, isn't she just a chick who got knocked up?"

Maria closed her eyes and flicked her tongue across her top teeth. "We don't worship Mary in the way you think. We honor her. She's the Queen of Heaven." She flashed her eyes at me. "Is that what you think of your mother? She just got knocked up and birthed you, and now that you don't need her, she doesn't matter?"

"It's more like the other way around. Once she birthed me, I didn't matter. I've never met her."

Instead of mumbling "I'm sorry," and letting the conversation die, she blinked, as she'd heard I was adopted before.

"What about your adopted mom? We don't honor Mary just because of the birthing part; she raised Jesus, too."

"As far as she knows, up until I left for college, I was just another sweaty body taking up space in her house."

She took a breath as if to say something then blew it out.

"Just spit it out."

Her brown eyes met mine. "If you could meet your biological mom, would you want to? Do you hope she's well, wherever she is?"

We both held our breath for a second.

I let mine out first. "Okay so, ya got me, I give a crap about my mom. So?"

"Well, we see Jesus as the son of God and all of us are also God's children, so in a way, Mary is our mother too." My eyes squinted at her; she word-vomited in response: "A mom who…who won't….fail us." Her voice trickled off, mumbling the last part.

"Hmph."

I went home and looked up a bunch of stuff about Mary that day and decided that it made more sense than I gave Catholics credit for. Besides, I knew Mike and Eddie didn't treat women well, and their passion for defacing Mary and stuff probably just fueled that behavior even more.

Eventually, I even started talking to Mary, sometimes even lighting a candle in my room that I found at a thrift store. I never told Maria, but maybe she saw the candle peeking out from my closet door when she was over sometime, because one Friday she plopped down next to me in our senior capstone and set a little white paper bag on my desk.

"What is this?" I grinned, thinking it must be a cookie or candy or something, our shared love of sweets always being our top priority.

"A gift." She looked nervous.

"No food?" My grin faded.

She swallowed, "Nope."

"Okay…" I moved to open it but her hand reached out to clamp down over mine.

She whispered, "Would you mind…waiting until you're not in front of me to open it?" So, she was nervous. Weird.

"Uh…sure…"

I decided not to let myself open it until my visit with Doug the next day. At his door, I entered the incorrect code that tells him it's me and not the cops or an FBI spy or something. A few moments passed. I heard '80s music blasting from the upstairs right window. His bedroom. I entered the code again. The music stopped, and I heard the click of the door unlocking. I slipped through, locking it behind me, and moved to sit on his midcentury-modern, orange sofa. My eyes desperately skirted over all the abstract, colorful art covering nearly every inch of the walls to look toward a table covered with framed family photos. One was of a younger Doug, maybe in his 20s before he was leading robberies, his arm thrown around an even younger dude with a receding hairline and matching flower tattoo. They're standing in front of Louisiana State University, and their smiles are open-mouthed, Doug pointing to a piece of paper the younger dude is holding up. Must be his brother, Andrew, I thought.

One time when it was my turn to ask questions, I asked Doug, "Who's Andrew?", remembering a scrapbook I saw sprawled on the counter once with that name etched on it. Doug stared at me for a long time. So long that I finally said, "You don't have to answer, you know." But he quickly responded, "He was my brother." I caught the "was" and mumbled that I was sorry. He responded, smiling a little, "You sometimes remind me of him."

I hastily changed the subject.

Later when I was back home, I felt like kicking myself for being a coward and copping out. Maria wouldn't have been a coward.

I shook my head as if to free myself of the memory and looked to the left of the couch. Standing there, as if it was naturally part of the room, was a Little Free Library complete with a stand and a tiny house-looking box painted bright blue and neon green. I darted over and pulled at the makeshift knob. Staring back at me were a ton of little crocheted animals, the frontmost one being a yellow octopus sticking its tongue out. I remembered Doug saying he has a secret business to pay the bills. I assumed it was probably selling something illegal. I laughed and closed the tiny door. Doug descended the spiral staircase from his bedroom in a white undershirt too small to cover his rather round beer belly and SpongeBob boxers.

"I see you found my famous Crochet Critters."

"Uh...yeah. So...Maria got me something."

"She did, did she? What did she get ya?"

I took the bag out of my pocket, "I haven't opened it yet."

"Why not?"

"Because whatever it is made her visibly nervous."

"Interesting...I assume you wanna open it now?"

"Yeah..."

"Okay...well...can you hurry up? I wanna continue my dance party."

I sighed. Doug tried to rearrange his face into a mask of boredom but his torso was leaning forward so much I thought he'd fall off the rainbow chair he'd sunk into. I smirked and turned the bag upside down, shaking the item inside onto my palm. Doug leaned forward some more.

He grunted, "It's a…bracelet?"

"Um…kind of?" It was made of dark leather and had several tiny knots looped along the band. I counted them absently at first and then with a thought in mind. "There are 10 knots…."

"Ah." Doug leaned back into the chair, his mask of boredom slipping off entirely, "What does that mean?"

"I think it's a decade rosary."

Doug squinted at me like I was speaking another language. "Like…an ode to the '80s?"

"What?" I shook my head not even knowing where to start. "No. You know Catholics pray what's called a Rosary? This is just a wearable, shorter version of that."

"Oh! Yes. The beady thing. I get it." He leaned forward while I twisted it onto my wrist. "So…you like it?"

"No…" I loved it. He knew I did. We talked for a long time that night. I admitted to praying to Mary. I wish I had a picture of Maria's face when I rolled up my sleeves one day, and she saw the bracelet hanging freely from my right wrist.

It's now 3:00 a.m., and I'm still contemplating all the ways my life could be ruined in a little less than six hours when I meet with the dean and he undoubtedly deems me guilty. I wonder if Doug is awake. This situation screams, "Break the rules and pay him a visit on a Monday morning for once."

At his door, I enter the incorrect, secret code, and he unlocks the door almost immediately, as if he was expecting me. I slip through, locking it behind me, and move to sit in my usual spot on the couch. Doug's already in his rainbow chair, crocheting something out of neon orange fabric. Of course.

He looks at me over a pair of obnoxiously large reading glasses, "Well, this is out of routine."

"Hey, Doug."

"Hey, Char."

"I can't sleep."

"Why not?"

"Tulane thinks I decapitated their statue of the Virgin Mary."

"That sounds messy."

"And it's not just any statue. It's this really important pilgrimage statue that only comes to Nola every few years or so." He sets his masterpiece down on the table. I start to feel like I'm stuck inside a skittle.

"I thought ya stopped vandalizing."

"I did."

"So, just tell them that."

"The statue was decapitated Saturday night. Between the hours of midnight and 5:00 a.m."

"Oh."

"Yeah."

"What are you going to tell them?"

"I thought maybe you could help me with that."

"Tell them you were at Café du Monde?"

"But couldn't the managers prove I wasn't?"

"What managers? Ya think the staff notices who's sitting on a table surrounded by vomit at 3:00 a.m. on Saturdays? Why do ya think I go there?"

"I guess that's a good point. But aren't there cameras? Something? The waiters know me. What would be worse? Me confessing to a crime I didn't do or making up an alibi that could be proven false, deeming me obviously guilty? Maybe I should just run."

"Well, I could definitely help ya out there." Doug laughs. I blink.

"Doug, I gotta finish college. I promised my adopted dad that I wouldn't be like the rest of our stupid family: just die on the farm they were born on and call it a day."

"Sounds nice to me."

"Coming here was a mistake. I'm gonna go home and keep whispering questions into the void. 'Doug's Skittle World' is making me nauseous."

Doug doesn't respond; I notice now he's looking at that same picture of Andrew I've stared at before. As I slip through the wooden door to Dauphine Street, Doug whispers from his cracked front door, "'Doug's Skittle World', huh? Sounds fun!"

"Bye, Doug."

"Mr. James, I owe you a formal apology."

"What? You say you owe me an apology?"

"Yes. We received a confession at 7:00 a.m. this morning."

"Oh. Wow. Was it Mike and Eddie?"

The dean blinks. "You're dismissed, Mr. James. Good luck in your studies this week."

I all but run out the door and head toward the one class left between me and graduation: critical theory. I sit down in my usual spot against the back wall of the classroom.

Maria sits down in her usual spot next to me. "Hey, Char. I heard about the confession, and I'm really sorry about what I said on our Sno-La tour. I know my apology doesn't change anything—"

"Look, Maria, it's fine. Let's just forget the whole thing—"

"No, it's not fine. I was wrong to corner you. I promise I won't mistrust you like that again."

Our professor calls our attention to the front of the room as class is starting, and I feel myself beaming up at him like an idiot.

Later, *The Tulane Hullabaloo* posts an article stating that the Mary Decapitator has been apprehended, and their identity is being withheld by police until further notice.

It's the kind of rainy day where you're not sure if the sun ever really rose, and Maria asks if I want to finish the new season of our favorite show we've been dying to watch. We doze off watching, and when I wake, it's 1:00 a.m. and the rain has slowed to a light drizzle. Maria's head is on my shoulder, her black curls covering most of her face. I think about kissing the top of her head then shake my head so fast I hear my neck pop. Maria sits up, startled, and piles her hair on top of her head, avoiding looking at me. I tell her I'm tired and want to head to bed, but in reality, I can't wait to tell Doug about the confession.

When I leave, I have every intention of catching the trolley to the Quarter, but I find myself standing in front of the chapel on Tulane's campus instead. They announced yesterday that they were holding perpetual adoration, and that there'd be security stationed out front. Inside, right in front of the altar, stands the decapitated statue: caution tape, severed head and all. I suck in a breath and contemplate bolting. There are a couple of people in the pews up front: one of them is an elderly man who looks to be silently crying, the other is a boomer-looking-lady kneeling and praying the Rosary. She looks back as the door behind me swings closed. I grimace and sit down in a pew in the very back. The silence feels heavy, like it's stuck. After a few deep breaths, I make myself look back up at the statue. Mary's rich red and gold crown is still attached, her eyes staring down the center aisle. Sheesh.

Her cheeks are framed by jagged pieces of her cream veil, as if the vandalizer struggled the most with hacking the veil apart enough to free her head. My mind starts to go numb as a heavy weight settles over me. I realize this whole time not once did I really care about the vandalism; I just cared about the trouble it might get me into. It wasn't that long ago that I was vandalizing myself, but I've been talking to

Mary a lot lately. Minutes pass. I get so lost in my thoughts I don't notice the elderly man leave and the boomer-looking-lady get up from her spot in the front and walk back to slide into my pew. She leans in and whispers, "Did you know that the first time this statue ever came to this city in the 1970s, it cried?" Great. She's one of those deep-dive-fake-news-Facebook-reading boomers. I make the snap decision to placate her a little:

"Um…it cried?"

"Yes!"

"Wow…" I can't look at her. Or the statue. I opt for staring at the ceiling instead and shove my hands in my jacket pockets.

She huffs out an amused breath and lowers her voice, "I'm not crazy. You can look it up. The statue actually cried. Human tears. There are photographs."

"Wow." I still haven't moved, except the slight shift of my eyes to the right corner of the ceiling: There's a little stain there. I figure if I stare at it long enough, she'll deem me a dud and leave.

She sighs, "I'll leave you alone. But, for some reason, I felt like I needed to tell you that." She smiles to herself, gets up, kneels, and leaves.

I continue to stare at that little stain on the ceiling for God knows how long. At some point, I realize I'm the only one in the chapel, and I remember Maria saying one time that during adoration you can't leave Jesus alone. Not even for a minute. I start to panic. Am I stuck here? Maybe I can beg the cop to come in: *Please sir, come inside. Jesus can't be alone, and I'm just a usually drunk college kid who likes to wander around in the middle of the night.*

The door opens and another young college dude walks in. I blow out an audible sigh of relief. He gives me a nod and slides into a pew a few rows ahead of me. Thank God. This is my chance to leave. I take a deep breath and hold it in, forcing myself to kneel and look at the statue. In my head, I spew a scrambled prayer: *Mary, I'm sorry. I real-*

ly am. All I cared about was getting out of this mess. Now I'm free to graduate, and you're, well, still headless.

I wince. Idiot choice of words.

I force myself to continue: "If it's true that this statue of you cried one time here, I bet it's 'cause of people like me. And Doug. And Mike. And Eddie. And most of the population." I pause, not quite knowing how to word it.

Then I rush it out: "People who are lost." I suddenly get up, my movement making the college dude whip his head around. But, I don't care. I stand in the center aisle. Help us to have the courage to stop wandering. I turn and leave without a second glance and walk straight for the Saint Charles trolley to the Quarter.

I can't wait to tell Doug that the vandalizer confessed, but when I slide through the wooden door to the courtyard, caution tape is strung across the front of Doug's apartment. I run up to his door and punch the code. Silence. I punch it again. Nothing. I slam my fist against the door repeatedly. I desperately punch the code one more time. I'm almost ready to scream his name regardless of who hears when a tiny piece of paper juts out from a hidden slot above the keyhole. I look behind me. The courtyard is completely empty save the light coat of rain across the cobblestone. I hold my breath as I read:

Charmon,

I don't know if you will already know by the time you get this note, but I confessed to decapitating the statue. Don't worry, I thought long about it. You're innocent and a senior close to graduating. You've got so much ahead of you. I've had my fun, 34 more years of it than I was supposed to. It's time to finish what I started.

Thanks for the laughs,
Doug

P.S. Ask Maria out. It's the least you can do. I just saved your butt.

I read the note at least 12 times before tearing it into tiny pieces, throwing them into the courtyard, and letting them settle into the damp cobblestone, dissolving in the rain. I kick the idiotic decaying wooden door in on my way out. I wander down Dauphine Street. A tarot card reader begs me to sit down and let her suck out some of my soul, and I have to bite down on my lip so hard it bleeds to keep from screaming at her. Screaming my throat out until the inside of it feels like raw meat.

Thirty-four years. Thirty-four years this man hid from the FBI and an idiot drunk senior in college who wanders around every Saturday night is worth giving it all up to him. What on earth do you call that? Compassion? Or insanity?

I don't even know where I'm walking, but somehow I end up at Café Du Monde. I sit down at a table and just stare into space. A waiter comes up and asks me if I want my usual, and I just stare at her too. She blinks and walks away muttering something about how they all go crazy eventually. A girl sits down at my table. I think about how she must be brave or maybe she's crazy herself and then I focus in on a hand waving in front of my face.

"Char. Char. Hello. Charmon James!" I blink. Maria continues, "Tell me what happened. Please, I just want to help."

I start, "How did you know…?"

"*Find my Friends,*" she smiles sheepishly. I don't respond for a while. Maria waits patiently. She must sense I need a few minutes, even more than five this time, if I'm ever going to say anything at all.

"He confessed."

"Who?"

"Doug."

"Who's Doug?"

I sigh. "I'll have to explain some other time." More silence.

"This Doug dude. He didn't do it, did he?"

"No."

"And neither did you."

It isn't a question but I nod anyway.

She starts to reach her hand across the table but then lets it fall into her lap. "I'm sorry, Char. Is there anything at all I can do?"

A few more minutes pass. I turn to stare at a street artist on the corner. She's painting a young woman, maybe a younger version of herself, dancing in the middle of an empty floor. Her movement looks crazy like she doesn't care that her arms are flailing and her head's spinning around and she just looks free. I think of that ridiculous '80s song Doug was listening to when I brought Maria's gift over. Doug's Skittle World.

"Maria, there is something you can do."

"What is it?"

I take a deep breath and hold it in. "Will you pray with me?'

She raises her brows, but nods subtly. And we pray. Right there in the middle of Café Du Monde. For Doug. And I swear the street artist starts mumbling along, as if absent-mindedly joining us.

When we're finished, I slip my rosary back on my wrist and continue to fidget with it, desperate to give my hands something to do. "Maria, there's something else."

"Anything, really." Her voice is soft.

"Ya gotta go out with me." She laughs. I'm still staring at my wrist, scared if I look up all my bravado will turn to mush. "That is, if you want to."

OLD COFFEE POTS AND NEW BEGINNINGS

Judy D'Ammasso Tarbox

The Distance Between Us

"Okay, chin down. Roll that neck around. Slowwwly. Now come back to center. Deep breath in. Hold it. Slowly let it go. That's it. Now shake out your hands. Great job! I'll open the chat. Tell me how it went."

I dutifully typed in the chat, *Thanks, Irene. It was great*, resisting the urge to add a sarcasm emoji. Not because Irene wasn't lovely, but because I was having yet another morning of guided stretching led by someone I'd never met in real life.

Then, as usual, I clicked Leave Meeting and closed my laptop before I got pulled into the black hole of virtual small talk.

I sighed and looked down at Max, my golden retriever and ever-faithful quarantine buddy, who was butting his head under my hand with his insatiable desire for pets and affection.

"Well, Max," I sighed, rubbing behind his ears, "it's been two years since the pandemic was officially pronounced over, and I'm still working, exercising, even having prayer and reflection time at home online most of the time. What a bust."

"Woof," he replied with great conviction.

"You agree, I see." I stood up, a bit more slowly than I'd like to admit for someone in her mid-thirties. "Let's go for our run. It's a bit chilly, so I'll grab a fleece. Maybe movement will jostle my sense of purpose back into place."

It was a cold but beautiful Saturday morning—sunny enough to pretend it was warmer than it actually was. I tugged on my fleece and collected Max's harness and leash when my phone buzzed from inside my pocket. I fished it out and saw my cousin Douglas's name lighting up the screen.

"Hello?" I answered, one eyebrow already raised. "What's up, Douglas?"

He never called this early on a Saturday. Not unless he'd accidentally signed up for a 5K in his sleep. Granted, he had started running a bit, short jogs in the park near his house, but still, it was suspicious. Very suspicious.

"Teresa, can we talk? I mean, in person. I need to run some stuff by you before a... meeting...this afternoon."

I narrowed my eyes at the phone like it could reveal what kind of "meeting" required hush-hush tones on a Saturday morning.

"You have a meeting on a Saturday?"

"Yeah," he said, with a hesitation that set off my internal cousin-speak translator.

"Work?"

More hesitation. Never a good sign.

"Not really... at least not traditionally."

"Well, that's reassuring," I said. "You sound confused."

"Well. Not confused, really. Cautious. The meeting is with some old high school friends talking about a possible reunion."

I glanced at Max, who had flopped over dramatically, as if this phone call was cutting into his scheduled emotional support run.

"I don't see what this has to do with me, Doug, but of course, we can talk. I'm just about to leave for my run, but I should be back within the hour."

"Thanks, cuz," he said, a blend of relief and wariness in his voice. "Anything you need? I mean, as long as I'm coming."

"Yes," I said, grinning. "How about stopping by the bagel shop and picking up an Everything bagel with low-fat garden veggie cream cheese on your way over?"

Doug laughed. "Not exactly a low-carb breakfast, now, is it, Teresa girl?"

I sighed.

"No, but we're in a holiday season... kind of... right? Easter time? And besides, carbs don't count when someone else buys them. It's science."

"If you say so," Doug chuckled. "See you in about an hour."

"Will do."

I hung up, shook my head, and turned to Max.

"Not sure what that's about, really. But let's go. I'll find out soon enough."

Max gave me a look that said, *Finally*, as I stuffed my phone back in my fleece, leashed him up, and headed out the door for our ritual trot through Hudson Lake.

My go-to route? From my cozy little bungalow toward Mountain View Community College—my in-person workplace (such as it was these days)—then loop back down the Avenue of Pines and finish along Spring Run Trail to home.

How many solitary runs along this route had I taken since I first arrived in Hudson Lake, right before the pandemic shut everything down? Too many. And I still didn't see any familiar faces.

Oh well, at least I had the trail. And the trail had me—panting, sweating, occasionally tripping over Max's leash—but committed.

I'm basically a slightly shorter, female version of my dad, Colin Parker, who was the reason I started running in the first place. And that's important, why?

At not-quite 5'5", I had the Parker family running instinct, along with the physical characteristics of green eyes with those weirdly charming hazel flecks, and sandy brown hair that had just enough strawberry-blonde in it to make people ask, "Do you dye it?"

I don't. It just grows that way, thank you very much.

My one issue—and it's a big one—is that I inherited my mother's Italian build.

Not the glamorous Sophia Loren kind.

Nope. I got the Maria Josephine Bianco Parker edition: petite.

Unfortunately, I only got half the package. While my mom and her side of the family were tiny, espresso-powered dynamos who could inhale three bowls of *pasta e fagioli* and still look like garden gnomes, I just had to smell it to gain two pounds.

So, I ran.

Partly because of Dad.

Mostly because of lasagna.

"I love good food," I've said more times than I can count, "so this is the price I pay. I should probably do a regular 5K just to offset the Nutella."

But somewhere along the way, I actually started to enjoy the rhythm, the breathing, the peaceful, pine-scented trails of the northeast mountains.

This was my therapy. Well, that and carbs.

A Pilgrimage Born from Loneliness

Forty-five minutes later, I rounded the final stretch of Spring Run Trail, slowing to a jog as my app chimed in with my pace: 9 minutes per mile. Meh. Usually, I clock closer to 8, so I made a mental note to pick it up if I wanted to actually get back in next year's Spindrift Half.

I spotted Doug's car already in my spare parking spot in the driveway.

"Huh," I muttered. "Must be serious. He's early."

I walked inside and called out, "Hey, Cuzcuz! I don't smell coffee yet!"

Doug's voice floated from the kitchen. "I'm trying!"

I looked toward the kitchen area of my cozy Sears Catalog bungalow—the Starlight—and saw him frowning at my beloved retro percolator like it was a Rubik's cube sent straight from the devil.

No, I don't have Superwoman's X-ray vision to see through walls. The previous owner of the house had rehabbed it and took out all the dividing walls between the living room, dining space, and kitchen. It was fantastic—light and open. So I really could see Doug clearly, furrowed face and all.

"Well," he said, continuing to glare at the contraption, "if you had a normal coffee pot like the rest of civilization…"

I held up a hand. "Blasphemy. That percolator is vintage, Doug. It has character. Like me."

He gave me a look. "Your 'character' is about to give me third-degree burns."

"Just wait until you meet my new retro toaster. She bites."

I went over and gave him a kiss on the cheek. "I got this—you get the cups, silverware, and plates for the bagels, and have a seat," I pointed to the stool at the peninsula, "then talk to me while I get Max fresh water, a biscuit, and make the coffee."

"You are the best, Teresa. Don't let any guy tell you otherwise—or they'll have to answer to me. Well, and Jim, of course. Maybe?"

I stopped in my tracks. Exasperated, I said, "If you're here to try to get me back with Jim, forget it. That breakup was the only really good thing to come out of the pandemic."

"Now that you mention it, he would like that—to get back with you. He says. But I'm not inclined to talk you into that direction."

"Wait! How do you know he wants to get back with me?"

"I ran into him last night at the bowling tournament. He asked about you. Said he would love to get back with you again. He misses you…you know, all that junk."

I shook my head. "What did you say?"

"Not much, really. I was 'noncommittal,' but it worried me because you've been so isolated. I mean, getting back with that two-timing creep is not the direction I want for you. And I will be seeing him later at the reunion committee."

I nodded. "I totally agree about Jim. And is that the meeting you mentioned? Your reunion committee from high school?"

Doug nodded.

"Okay. Now the next red flag. If it's not Jim, what direction are you inclined to try to talk me into?" I asked cautiously.

"One that's good for your soul."

"And I thought you were going to say bowling."

"Nope. Not that, heaven forbid. Where you have to be out with real people. And touch things..."

"Okay, okay. But my soul? Sounds like you've also been talking to my mother!"

He smiled. "No. Just reading up on the Jubilee Year. And wondering if you're up for a pilgrimage?"

"A pilgrimage? You mean like going to Rome or someplace?"

"Rome would be great, but I'm thinking closer to home. Like the Cathedral of the Immaculate Conception in Albany."

"I... I never considered."

"Teresa," he said soberly, "it's time you moved on and out a bit! You've been pretty much holed up here in Hudson Lake since the pandemic hit."

I sighed and said reluctantly, "I know you're right. How about I think about it and let you know in a day or two?"

"I'm going to hold you to it, cousin. I know you're lonely. It's time to change that. You're my new job."

"As long as I don't have to pay you a salary. At least not in dollars. Will you take my homemade biscotti?"

"Since I get that now anyway, you have to throw in a cannoli or two."

"So, that's it? That's what you were so concerned about?"

"Yes. And that you might still have feelings for the jerk Jim." He shook his head. "The way he was talking last night... It worried me.

You deserve better. And I want to have a clear answer if I see him later."

"Thanks, cousin. You have nothing to worry about on that score."

"Promise?"

"Promise."

And we turned the conversation over to work, our families, the new woman in Doug's life (who, it turns out, is a great bowler), and then he left—leaving me alone with my thoughts about the Jubilee, pilgrimage, and expanding beyond my safe and cozy bungalow.

The First Step—Still Online but Progress Made

Skeptical but curious about Doug's suggestion, I decided to take my first steps toward learning about the Jubilee Year and how to make a pilgrimage. Naturally, the first thing that popped up was the idea of a virtual pilgrimage. Well...hey, you've got to start somewhere, right?

And I found out it was a thing. So, I made a plan.

Starting the next morning, I got up and said my prayers—okay, with the help of the *Hallow* app, but still. I also took a few minutes to journal before diving into my normal morning routine of coffee, a shower, and either sitting down at the computer or heading to campus for part of the day.

After a few days, I added lighting a candle during prayer time, focusing specifically on hope, mercy and forgiveness. I even decided to start showering and dressing first before prayer time. Something about not showing up in pajamas or a mangy sweatsuit gave the time a greater sense of respect and worship. (Not that I think God cares about my outfit—pretty sure He's just happy I showed up.)

I'd love to say everything went smoothly from there... but, well, real life has a way of kicking in.

There's my neighbor—the one who enjoys firing up power tools and lawn equipment at sunrise. I'm still not sure what he's doing, but it apparently requires the same amount of maintenance as the Pebble Beach Golf Course.

And then there's Max.

Max always seems to need to go out at the exact wrong time. Or he'd nudge my hand for petting mid-Rosary. I lost track of my beads more times than I can count.

But you know what? God is good. And forgiving. And somehow, even in all the chaos, something began shifting inside me.

It was the Rosary that really moved things to the next level.

Doug, who had been checking in with me almost daily, suggested trying a livestreamed Rosary hosted by Saint Mark's church in Albany—Doug's childhood family church.

That first night, it honestly felt a little like my online stretching group... except the focus was on internal stretching.

When the Rosary ended, I quietly signed off.

By the second week, something shifted.

I typed into the chat that I was grateful for the group. It was easing the loneliness that had clung to me for the past two years.

That's when someone reached out—Ed C., a fellow Hudson Lake resident. Turns out he lived just off the Avenue of Pines, on Maple Ridge Road. Right off my running route. Go figure. Coincidence? Or maybe divine intervention. Hmm.

I'm sorry your move to Hudson Lake has been so challenging, he typed. *Even though I haven't been here that much longer than you, we're really a very nice, welcoming community when there's not a pandemic in the way.*

Intrigued but cautious, I typed back a quick reply. Nothing major—just a friendly thanks and a comment about how nice it was to know there were real people actually living in Hudson Lake and not just appearing on the town website.

Over the next few days, Ed and I exchanged a few notes through the chat. Turned out we had a lot in common: living in the same town, dealing with the weirdness of making friends during a pandemic, and now fumbling our way through a virtual faith life. We even taught at the same college—he was History, while I was English. And he had a similar running route, just in the opposite direction. We shared pictures.

It felt...comfortable. Easy. Familiar.

I started looking for him running past me when I took my runs. No luck just bumping into him, though. Maybe I should tell him—subtly—the times I go.

Then one evening, after the Rosary ended and Max had already flopped over for his post-prayer nap, I opened my email and found a short message from Ed: *Would you like to meet for coffee sometime? We could bring the dogs. Public place, low pressure, and the caffeine's on me.*

I stared at the screen for a minute, my heart doing that awkward little two-step of excitement and panic.

Meet an almost-stranger for coffee? In person? With actual eye contact?

But also...coffee. And someone who actually seemed kind. And the chance to finally, maybe, feel a little less alone in Hudson Lake.

I smiled and started typing back. *Sounds good. Max votes yes, too.*

The Coffee Klatch Connection

The next day, I was nervous as I got ready for my...what? Meeting? Yes. He was paying, so—date? Kind of. Sort of. First date? Maybe.

I pulled on my black jeans, a white cotton shirt, and a black-and-white herringbone fleece jacket. Classic but comfortable.

"Ready, Max?" I looked down at my golden retriever. "Shadow's a golden-doodle mix, so you two should hit it off, right?"

Max cocked his head, tongue hanging out, looking as innocent as could be. His expression clearly read: *Of course. What did you think?*

We headed down our street toward town onto Main Street and there it was. The coffee shop I passed a hundred times on my walks and runs: The Coffee Klatch.

It was beautiful. Big windows overlooked the lake, and inside was a cozy woodstove with glass doors, so the fire was visible from all sides. Light maple tables and Windsor-style chairs filled the space, with a cluster of comfy wingback chairs gathered around an oriental rug near the stove. The oak floors gleamed under the soft light, and the ceiling was pressed tin with a weathered copper patina.

To one side, French doors led to an outdoor patio with seating and heating torches. You could also access it from the outside, which I did, not sure if dogs were allowed to pass through the inside.

Ed spotted me as Max and I approached. He stood, with a wide smile on his face, and extended his hand. Shadow jumped up and began sniffing Max, who sniffed right back.

"Looks like they're hitting it off," I said, smiling, my voice a little shaky as I took Ed's hand.

"Have you been here before?" he asked.

"Only once, I'm sorry to say," I replied, pulling my hand back awkwardly. "I ran in for a coffee to go when I didn't have Max with me. It's gorgeous inside."

He nodded, smiling. "And smells heavenly too. They roast their own beans. So delicious."

"I usually just drink a simple espresso latte... Unless you have a better recommendation?"

He laughed—a warm sound. "Espresso does it for me too. But here comes the waitress." He nodded toward the French doors leading inside. "She might have a suggestion."

We sat down, and soon a delightful conversation unfolded—about everything: our families, college days, teaching, and faith journeys.

"The pandemic changed me too," Ed said, shaking his head. "I was only at Mountain View Community College one semester before you. So, not a lot of time to get involved before we were shut down. Then after," he continued, "it was too easy to lock myself away and stay that way. Especially being new at the school. I never really got back into the social side of work. Still haven't."

"I know what you mean." I shook my head. "You go to some meetings, chat with people...but it's all surface-level. No real friendships. Just passing through and online semi-connections."

"Well," he smiled and cocked his head, "at least until the rosary group."

"How did you find out about the online rosary group?" I asked.

"St. Mark's is my home parish. One of my old high school friends reached out to me about it. You might know him—Douglas Parker? We're actually on a high school reunion committee together."

"You're kidding, right?" I said—and then it hit me. To Ed C., I was Teresa P.

"We never even asked each other our last names!" I exclaimed, astonished it had never occurred to me.

He grinned. "I know. Probably not the smartest move, but I figured, hey, we met through an online rosary group from Saint Mark's. And you didn't strike me as a dangerous person. Quite the opposite, actually." He raised a hand before I could speak. "For the record, my full name is Edward Francis Coletti."

I laughed, feeling a wave of relief. "So it was the talk about Nutella and cannoli that pulled you in?"

He nodded, still smiling. "Among other things."

I decided it was my turn. Grinning, I said, "Ed, you might find this interesting...I think we've been set up."

"Set up?"

"My full name is Teresa Josephine Parker."

Surprise lit up his face. "Are you telling me...?"

"My cousin is Douglas Patrick Parker. Your old high school friend and reunion buddy."

"Well, I'll be!" Ed looked astonished. Then, shaking his head, he said, "Remind me to thank him profusely."

I grinned. "While I am glad he was persistent, I'm not sure thanking him is what I'll do! The sneak! I don't want to encourage him, that's for sure."

"But, Teresa, be honest. If he told you what his motives were, would you have done the rosary group? Or the particular rosary group he picked out?"

Reluctantly, I said, "Probably not."

"So, along with wanting us to meet, he wanted us to begin a friendship—and a pilgrimage. A journey about going in the right direction. Finding forgiveness and hope, along with friendship and community to help us on this journey."

"You're right," I said softly. "When you put it that way, I guess I do need to thank him. Eventually."

Now Ed laughed, a hearty, genuine sound. "I get the impression you want him to twist a little first."

"Just a touch."

And suddenly, I knew I was sitting across from someone who understood me and this new journey we were beginning together.

He gets it, I thought, and felt lighter than I had in years.

A New Kind of Pilgrimage

Over the next few weeks, I met Ed online and at the coffee shop. Sometimes we brought the dogs; sometimes not. Of course, Max always pouted when I left without him.

"Sorry, boy. You'll come next time."

He never believed me.

When we went dogless, we sat at the same corner table inside and discussed the readings we were making for the Jubilee. Our own private book group. Or book pair?

"Your usual?" Ed would always say, with a warm smile. "I actually like saying that."

"I kind of like it too."

We kept each other accountable to continue live and in-person and met at the 8:00 a.m. Mass every Sunday at All Saints Church right in Hudson Lake.

Schedules didn't allow for live Eucharistic Adoration, but we found it online and spent solo time on our knees in our respective living rooms, then shared our thoughts online. Hey, we couldn't quit the virtual cold turkey.

The same went for our rosary group. We continued to meet online with everyone else—including Douglas. The cad positively gloated at the friendship that was blooming between Ed and me.

As the spring weather took over, we added walks by the lake and quiet dinners at the Pine Tree Inn, whose restaurant included a wonderful deck over the water.

Our conversations were deep. The loneliness slowly went away. We even talked about starting a small, in-person book group because others might be feeling the same way.

Then we hit another milestone. Early one Saturday morning, my doorbell rang. Max started barking and jumping excitedly, looking out the front window.

I stood on tiptoes, and sure enough, through the glass panes I saw Ed, holding up a bag from our favorite bagel place, smiling.

I threw open the door. "What a happy surprise."

"I'm glad you think so," he said, grinning sheepishly. "It's such a beautiful morning, I thought we could picnic at the lake."

"Or you can come in and picnic in my kitchen."

"You sure?"

I nodded and smiled. "Yes. And I just made a pot of coffee."

"Great. I didn't think I could carry the bagels, the dog's leash, and the coffee, so I just have a water bottle stuck in my backpack—along with napkins and cream cheese, of course. Light Garden Veggie, to be exact. Besides, I want to finally see the great coffee dragon."

"You've been talking to Douglas," I said, shaking my head as we headed to the kitchen area.

"Great place," he said, looking around. "Such an open, comfortable space."

"Thanks," I said, pouring the coffee while Ed turned toward the peninsula and put down the bag of bagels. Shadow and Max curled up beside us like two best buds.

Ed took the cup I offered, sipped, closed his eyes for a moment, and gave a slow, appreciative nod.

"Okay," he said, smiling. "Douglas was wrong. This coffee is worth the risk."

I laughed, feeling lighter than I had in a long time. "Thank you. Some things are better the old-fashioned way."

Ed glanced around the house, then back at me. His voice was a little softer. "You know... it's really nice here. Warm. Feels like people should be gathering around in this space."

I hesitated, feeling the weight of the past few years—the long months of quiet, the cautious steps back into community. I never realized the extent of my pandemic isolation until now.

"Funny you should say that," I said, sliding a plate toward him. "I've been thinking about the expanded book group we've talked about. Not online. In person. Here. At my house."

Ed's face lit up. "That sounds great, Teresa. Exactly what people need. And we can start small. Doug of course and his new love Penny, along with Josh and Katie, from church."

I nodded and added excitedly, "I'm thinking we can add Marian Consecration to our pilgrimage—how about *33 Days to Morning Glory*? I know Marian Consecration isn't officially part of the Jubilee, but it's recommended as a personal spiritual act."

Ed's face brightened. "I read that many dioceses are encouraging Marian Consecration. I'm sure Father Tom will help us. So, what can I do to help?"

And for the next couple of hours, we pored over my laptop, planning dates, materials, and everything we needed for an exciting and important study.

When we finished, our four friends were already on board, and we were ready to commit Friday evenings at my place for food, fellowship, and prayer.

Looking into my eyes, Ed lifted his coffee cup in a mock toast.

"To old coffee pots and new beginnings."

A Pilgrimage of Hope—Or Coming 180 Degrees

Over the next few weeks, we met and worked with some preliminary reading material. By August, we had started our main book—33 Days to Morning Glory—so our consecration day would fall on the Feast of the Assumption.

We got into a rhythm, starting the evening with easy crock-pot or casserole meals (of course, my homemade lasagna was in the lineup—requested by Ed and Doug), make your own subs, or make your own pizza, along with salad. Totally casual, but perfect Friday-night fare.

Then, with fresh, hot coffee from my trusty old percolator and a sweet treat to go with it, we settled into the living room and began with an opening prayer, which included our weekly intentions. From there, Ed and I led the book discussion.

Along the way, something beautiful unfolded.

Spiritually, we all grew closer to the Blessed Mother—and through her, deepened our relationship with Jesus—experiencing growth not just in faith, but personally and emotionally as well.

Ed and I discovered we made a great team, working together in sync and really understanding each other. As a group, we found a renewed sense of community and hope.

And just as meaningful—at least to me—was that the brew from my old coffee pot won everyone over. Even Douglas. Turns out, perked coffee can hold its own in the 21st century world of coffee innovation. Validation.

We also discovered there was another small group in our church doing the same book, so we stayed in touch with them. We didn't expand the groups—we liked the intimacy of the smaller numbers—

but we coordinated and prepared to have a mutual consecration ceremony. It made life easy for Father Tom, too, who was excited to host this at our little "country" church.

When the day came, we had confession and held a special Mass on Saturday morning with just the two groups and a few family members. We recited the consecration prayer together—thank goodness, because my voice was trembling. Then each of us placed a rose at the statue of the Blessed Mother in the Grotto on the church grounds. We prayed the Chaplet of Divine Mercy and had time for quiet prayer and reflection.

The next day, Sunday, we made our way to the late-morning Mass at the Cathedral of the Immaculate Conception in Albany, one of the officially designated sites for the Jubilee year, and completed our pilgrimage. Our journey as "Pilgrims of Hope" came to a close.

When it was over, everyone returned to my house for one last treat of Italian pastries and of course coffee.

It seems I'm slowly creating a buzz—not just for consecration, pilgrimage, and renewed hope and community, but for percolated caffeine.

After it was over, Ed suggested we take a walk by the lake and enjoy what was left of the day. I should have known something was up when he indicated we leave Max and Shadow behind. "They'll be fine outside in the fenced-in yard with plenty of water," he said, selling the idea.

We walked down to the beach, holding hands as we made our way to our favorite spot—a place that looked out over the quiet expanse of the lake, where the rays of the sun, sinking lower in the sky, danced across the gentle waves. We sat on a bench, and Ed reached into his pocket, pulling out a small necklace box.

He smiled, held it out to me and said softly, "To remember our first pilgrimage."

"Does that mean there will be more?"

"That's a positive—at least on my end."

I smiled. "On my end too." I opened the box to find a beautiful silver Miraculous Medal.

I leaned in and softly kissed him, tears stinging my eyes, knowing our pilgrimage hadn't ended. In so many ways, it had only just begun.

THE PROMISE

A.R.K. Watson

Bishop Miki was dying.

He knew he was but he didn't know how he knew. It was hard to think clearly through the fever, but the fact remained he was dying and he was dying a failure.

The walls of the mud hut around him dripped with moisture but he didn't mind. It was easier to breathe inside the hut. His body still shivered despite the heat. The door to the hut was made of woven strands of grass and a fibrous blue freshwater weed the colonists called "blue river grass." Such a bland name for such an uncommon thing, but this world was too full of uncommon things to waste time trying to appropriately name each one.

The green light of a four-moon night glinted soft through the weave of the door. He'd gotten those right at least. As the head astronomer the colonists let him name anything in the sky. He'd named them for his four favorite authors; Chesterton was big and comically pitted and shaped, like a ball of dough kneaded by a child's hands. Flannery was quick and sharp, spinning on a rotation twice the speed of the others. Tolkien was the closest and spotted with green craters, looking as if it were a fae land just out of reach. Endo was the smallest, its rotation far-flung and often in darkness, before appearing out of nowhere on a schedule he still hadn't worked the kinks out of mathematically. Not that it mattered. His astronomer's career had only ever been a means to an end, the means to get him accepted into one of Japan's few slots for the Martian colony. The Vatican had kept his bishopric secret until after he'd been established there. His native country had allowed freedom of religion for hundreds of years now, but sending up the first Catholic bishop wasn't their PR move of choice.

He sighed and had to smother another bout of coughing. He knew his apprentice was sitting just outside, and he didn't want to lose the boy any more sleep than he had these past few nights. Teaching the young Villalobos boy had been an exercise in joy and grief. Joy because Benito was so full of curiosity and excitement about learning from him, and grief because Bishop Miki had had to rethink his profession so thoroughly. On Mars he'd had the latest technology and tools. But ever since fate had washed them ashore on this nameless planet, they were barely more than overly-educated cavemen. Even this sweat lodge, with its campfire pit in the center and circular stone slabs for beds around it, was an ancient folk medicine revived by the colonist's PhD doctors.

Luckily this planet didn't seem all that hostile to humans. Besides them and a strange lemur-like species the colonists called Leoples (shortened from little peoples), the planet seemed utterly empty of animal and insect life. The illnesses that came were usually brief and mild. Even this fever he had only lasted three days in most people. But he knew he wouldn't see the end of it. He'd dreamed of this death a year ago, its details so clear and exact there had been no mistaking it.

Bishop Miki didn't get prophetic dreams often. Before this one, he'd had one other. One crisp Martian morning, he'd woken up with the clear image of his mother embracing him, and then turning to walk into the light. He'd known even before he saw the message his brother had sent him that their aging mother had died suddenly in her sleep in her small apartment in Nara prefecture. Though she'd been old, she'd been in good health and everyone was taken aback by it. Bishop Miki had only sat through the Buddhist ceremonies, streamed up to him via the entangled network that kept Mars and Earth connected, silent and numb.

His mother, on the other hand, seemed to have had multiple such dreams. With no family history of hallucinations or delusions, and too many coincidences to explain, Bishop Miki had long ago accepted this strange part of his mother's life.

He didn't think it would happen to him, especially after he left Buddhism.

The dream had been a warning, he knew that now, a last-ditch chance for him to rectify his mistake before an entire planet of people was left adrift and alone in space. He'd tried. He really had. He'd made Abayomi a priest. He'd been a married man, but Bishop Miki saw little use in enforcing a rule of celibacy on a colony that so desperately needed more children. Abayomi had been a good man, serving as deacon under him for five years before taking final vows, and then found gorged to death by a meadow brush within a week of saying his first Mass. He'd left a wife and five children, all girls. Two of them would, no doubt, join Maria Villalobos in her small convent outside the village walls. When he was dead, the village Catholics would have her small group of sisters to look to for baptisms, weddings, and anointing of the sick, but nuns could not perform any other rites, not the most important one.

Bishop Miki rubbed his eyes.

"*Kamisama, cocoromidata,*" he groaned. But God knew. God knew too about Fr. Hugo, but Bishop Miki didn't like to think about Fr. Hugo.

He should have done more, he knew. They'd been on this lost planet now ten years but so much of the early years had been about just surviving. It had been hard for even him to think about more than just food and shelter. And then as life settled down, he would talk sometimes at Mass of the need to continue the line of Peter, to keep the old rites alive, these things that seemed like the last elements tying them to Earth, as much as to God. But none had come forward until Abayomi. Too many of them, he knew, shared Fr. Hugo's doubts.

For some years he'd wrestled with them himself, though he'd kept that a shameful secret. Bishop Miki watched his hands shake in his lap and wanted to laugh but was too tired. *What use was a secret now?* he thought. Only another year in purgatory if he was lucky. There would be no one to say Mass for his soul when he was gone.

Outside the door, the wind blew, briefly swinging the door flap open a bit, and he had a glimpse of Ben sitting against the lodge wall, a stylus in hand and a large charting scroll open on his lap. Ben's smooth cheeks, puckered in that manner he had when he was calculating. The sight warmed Miki's heart. Ben had this harebrained idea that he was going to find Earth's sun one day, figure out where it was they'd ended up in space. Miki never had the heart to disabuse him of the idea but what he was talking about was something that had never been done in all of human history. The constellations changed slightly when viewed from Mars but they were still recognizable. Back in the Sol galaxy, astronomy was useful because it was so consistent. That consistency was what made it a useful skill for travelers exploring the surface of Earth. But on this planet, none of the stars were recognizable.

It was what had broken Hugo in the end.

Bishop Miki shook his head. Benito wasn't like Hugo. It was a small community, but he and Hugo still managed to avoid each other. When he did see his old fellow priest, the man was usually drunk, though, oddly, he didn't think the man had ever broken his vow of celibacy. But where was he now? And what other eighteen-year-old would have spent this week caring for an old childless man like him?

What if he asked Ben? No, he pushed the thought away. Benito was kind and eager but he was much too young to take on the priesthood. And then there was that troublesome way he looked down on his twin brother for marrying young rather than finish his education. Yes, passing on the knowledge was important but really what use would astronomy be here? Maybe at best, the colony would grow enough to send out further expeditions and map the whole planet but that would be long after both he and Ben were gone. No, no. Maybe if he'd had more time he could have helped Ben be ready for such a task but it would be unfair to ask him of it now, and so suddenly.

Bishop Miki's head swam and gingerly he laid down to sleep, and began to dream.

He stood once again in the grove of Whistle Trees downriver. They weren't really trees but they were tall, white pillars with holes that formed in just such a manner that faint mellow tones sounded when the wind blew through them. Fr. Hugo stood across from him, leaning against one such pillar, arms crossed.

"I can't lie to them anymore, Bishop," Hugo said. His eyes were red. Had he been crying? How had he not noticed then?

"What lie, son?" he'd said then but, in the dream, he only regarded the other man silently.

"We are supposed to trust in God because he keeps his promises. That's how the stories go, isn't it? Even back to Judaism, God makes a promise and then we see Him keep it, each promise fulfilled, each covenant made, revealing something more to us about God's nature and His plan for the world. And then there is us, the Catholics." He sighed and tried to smile. "'You are rock and upon this rock I will build my church and the gates of hell will not overcome it.' And we are supposed to trust that our great big institution of frocked men will never fail to have a line of successors."

"Yes, Hugo, we are those successors."

"Are we?" Hugo had asked, bitterness building in his eyes, a bitterness that Miki had never seen, and would never see him without again, the bitterness that Hugo would drink to dull away.

"And you, Bishop? Are you in communion with Rome? When are you planning your ad limina trip the Eternal City?"

"We aren't the only ones waiting, Hugo," Miki had begged. "The Rabbi still says, 'Next year in Jerusalem.' The Imam is recording all the names of the Muslims for the one who will one day carry the scroll to Mecca on their behalf."

Hugo shook his head. "It's not the same and you know that," Hugo said.

This was when the tears began to flow in earnest from Hugo's eyes. The memory Miki had been startled. The dream him watched silent, as if watching them from behind a Whistle tree, and wondered how many tears his old friend had shed before he'd found the courage to speak to him about this.

"It's done. No more priests. No church. No God." Hugo sucked in a sharp breath and closed his eyes. "They'll all realize it soon enough," he whispered.

Miki's eyes opened, heart hammering in his chest, and began another of his coughing fits. He barely registered the sound of the door opening, the feet that pounded the dirt floor, until Ben was lifting him up, making sure he did not fall into the fire pit in his fit.

"It's okay, Father," Ben murmured. "I've got you."

Miki gazed bleary-eyed at the young man and felt his heart thrum with gratitude. He didn't deserve Ben's kindness. And that kindness—that love—that should count for something, shouldn't it? Love could cover over a multitude of faults. And there would be time for someone young as him to learn. Like how, in a marriage, a young couple grew with each other, learning to adapt to the other's foibles.

"Ben-kun," Miki said as he regained himself, "I need to ask you. I'd—I'd hoped you would come to me in your own time, when you felt ready, but it can't wait any longer."

"What is it, Shikyou?"

"Will you take the vow?" he said, reaching out his palm to place it on his student's forehead. But his student drew back, confusion on his face.

"Benito-san," said Bishop Miki, "Will you take on the priest-hood?"

Ben seemed frozen for a moment and then his eye widened. The young man tried to stand and bumped his head on the low ceiling of the sweat lodge. Flecks of clay crumbled and fell into his straight black hair and down the neck of his poncho.

"What? You're not serious?" Ben cried.

"This village must have a Shikyou, Benito-san," Miki pleaded.

Ben shook his head.

"Not me. It doesn't need me. I'm only eighteen. *Merde!* I haven't even had a proper girlfriend yet! I—I'm not even done with school!"

"You don't need to have finished school to become a priest."

"I've studied astronomy, not theology!"

"You know more of it than most of the villagers."

"I—I," the young man stuttered and started backing away to the exit. "You're not thinking clearly. *Sólo estoy diciendo.* You'll regret saying any of this tomorrow morning." Ben drew away and folded the door back into its groove behind him.

Bishop Miki collapsed on the stone again, too weak to move.

"*Kamisama,*" he gasped. "*Yotei wa nandesuka?*" and fell into another stupor.

His next dream felt different.

He floated in the main cabin of a ship. He didn't know how he knew it was a ship. The walls were green, and coated in small leaves and budding fruit. The close air smelled like lychee fruit and human sweat. A man with long brown hair and beard sat on the floor in the center, his arms outstretched, eyes closed as if in meditation. Two thin vines seemed to grow out of the crooks of the man's arms, like strange IV lines, but Miki could not tell if the vines were sucking the man's blood or feeding him its sap.

"We're almost there," the man murmured, and with a start, Miki recognized that voice. It was Ben, but a grown Ben, older, lined but not yet graying. Miki looked around, his heart beating hard. The clarity, the smell. It was like the dream of his mother's death, like the dream of his own. But he wasn't yet dead, was he? Had he died in his sleep? Miki put a hand to his chest and felt, faintly as though from far away, a pain that thrummed up from his heart and through his left arm. Pain was good, wasn't it? Dead men didn't feel pain.

Somehow comforted, he turned back to Ben sitting on the floor. His eyes moved underneath closed eyelids like he was seeing something, controlling something?

Miki turned around and saw at the other end of the ship, three other figures asleep on the floor. One was Ben's older sister but the others had their heads tucked into their sleeping packs too deep to see their faces.

He saw then the stole sitting folded on a pile of supplies in the corner. His stole—a relic of his life, carried here by his student.

The dream shifted and the strange ship disappeared around him. Benito stood in the great halls of Saint Peter's, his eyes cast upwards into the dome of the church, his hands clutching Miki's stole.

"We made it, Father," Benito whispered, the light of Earth's sun upon his face.

Then the dream dissolved back into the haze of regular sleep.

When Miki opened his eyes again, he was looking down on his sleeping form lying on his stone bed. Ben stood over him, doing chest compressions.

"Please don't die!" Ben gasped, tears running down his face unheeded. "Don't leave us! I'm sorry, I'll take it! I'll be a priest, just don't leave us, Father!" he wailed.

Miki reached down to brush his student's head but though he felt his arm move, he could see no hand of his to touch anything with. His hands were there upon the stone. He didn't need them now. He'd be reunited with them again one day but for now he felt suddenly content to wait. Below him, Miki saw that Ben's hands had stopped moving, had given up, and the young man had collapsed, weeping on Miki's chest like a young child. He saw Ben's right hand close around the stole that hung from Miki's neck and the old bishop smiled.

"We will make the ad limina together," Miki promised him. "From wherever I am, I will pray and be with you on your journey."

The old bishop turned away from his student, and pausing a moment at the sight, stretched out his hands and ran into the light.

THE DAY THE DOME DROPPED ON MY HEAD

Mary McWilliams

Tara closed her laptop, feeling satisfied and content. Seconds before, she had authorized the down payment for her first pilgrimage. She intended it to be a reflective time to learn more about her Catholic faith, to which she recently returned and was still unsure if she even belonged. She also hoped it would provide some direction on the next part of her life. The tour promised visits to Vatican City, the Vatican Museum, Sunday Mass with the pope, a tour of the Appian Way, Saint John Lateran Basilica, daily Mass at a different historic church, and much more for only seven days. Maybe for her, like some pilgrims, a miracle might occur.

She'd heard about pilgrimages her whole life. She recalled distant relatives coming to call on her parents after returning from far-off places with prayer cards for her mother and stories about people and happenings Tara had never heard of. She didn't know what they did or saw, but they always spoke of it as a trip of a lifetime. After they left, her mother would sigh and say how much she longed to go to the same places. She never did.

Later in life, although she didn't practice her faith, Tara read more about popular pilgrimage sites and the miracles that took place. She understood why her mother had such a strong desire to go. She began to think it would be a lost dream for her too, and it might have been, if it weren't for her Uncle Cozzie. In only about a year, from his sick bed no less, Cozzie's influence through his quiet and regular prayers, his welcoming of priests and church visitors, and his gentle prodding to attend church, and the example of his own faith, Tara opened her heart again to God, returned to church, and was driven to learn more about her faith. Now, she had finalized plans for the pilgrimage.

"Thanks, Cozzie," she said, her hands resting on the laptop. "I miss you."

When Uncle Cozzie's son and daughter-in-law tried to put him in a nursing home as he was dying from congestive heart failure, Tara intervened and brought him to her home. Her cousins offered no resistance, just sloppy gratitude that Tara found embarrassing for them. Now her beloved uncle was in the same house and in the same room where she had cared for her father until he died, and her mother until she passed. Her father's brother, Cozzie, had been a lifelong devout Catholic. He kept a rosary and brown scapular on the bedpost so they would be within easy reach. Oftentimes, when Tara went to check on him, she found him in prayer.

Each morning, when she brought him coffee and toast, he sat on the edge of the bed, made the sign of the cross and spent a few seconds in silence before raising the cup, inhaling the strong coffee, and taking a sip.

"You make the best coffee, Tara," he said every time. She laughed.

"Well, only you and I know that, Cozzie, because no one else will drink it."

At night, before she tucked him in, she buttoned up his pajama top and brushed his hair while he recited the Saint Michael the Archangel and Guardian Angel prayers. Eventually, Tara joined him.

"Never forget to thank your guardian angel, Tara. He's helping in ways we don't know."

"Yes, Uncle," she'd reply.

Every so often, he'd ask if she were going to church that day.

"No, Cozzie. I haven't been to church in years."

"Why don't you go to church, Tara?" Uncle Cozzie would ask her gently. "Confession and Mass. It's important to be right with God."

"Right, Uncle," she'd agree.

When the priest came to visit Cozzie and offer Communion, he'd invite Tara to church or mention a Bible study or committee work she might enjoy. "We have a fairly strong Knights of Columbus chapter. I could find a couple of men to come kibbitz with Cozzie. Or maybe some ladies to dote on him," he'd offer so she could have some time to herself or participate in the church activities.

After several months of invitations, Tara said yes. Two days later, she was in a Bible study on 1 Corinthians, learning she really hadn't a clue what the Bible was about, or who Jesus Christ was and is. Now, she was beginning to understand. She wanted more. She ordered books by the author of the Bible study. She found more authors. Some demystified teachings of the Church. Others wrote of their conversion. Her favorite lessons taught historical and linguistic contexts. She loved hearing, "In the original Greek, the word means ..." Or "At that time in Jerusalem ..."

As Cozzie's condition worsened, his breathing became more labored and his memory dulled. Hospice was brought in. Tara continued to have support from the church people who appreciated their time with Cozzie as much as he did, and it allowed her to participate a bit more in church functions. Driving to and from church, she heard a commercial for a Rome pilgrimage.

"Gosh, I'd love to do that," she said to herself. "But it's not the right time." The trip was months away, but Cozzie was her priority. Was that why her mother never went on pilgrimage? Because someone else always came first?

On a February night, Cozzie seemed to become someone else. He'd already suffered memory loss from age and heart failure. But this night, it seemed to turn into a delirious state. As best as Tara could make out, Cozzie thought he was in an Army hospital during wartime. He kept ordering her to get a stretcher for the guy in the corner and complaining about no one helping the soldier.

She called the 24-hour hospice line asking to speak to his nurse, but the nurse on duty said to give him morphine to calm him down. Cozzie remained agitated, but he no longer thought he was in an Army hospital. He didn't seem to know Tara, either.

She called the hospice hotline again.

"It's been more than an hour, and he's no calmer," she told the nurse. "When is someone getting here?"

"Give him another dose of morphine," the nurse told him.

A second dose didn't help, and she still couldn't get him to stay in bed.

Tara called the hospice again.

Tara hadn't anticipated the difficulties of Cozzie's condition would escalate into mental episodes during which sweet, gentle Uncle Cozzie would turn into a combative soldier who didn't know her. His physical strength became more than would seem possible in his weakened state and more than Tara could handle by herself. If this was going to be the new standard, she would need help. Hours after the morphine finally took effect, the hospice nurse arrived.

"Every case is different. It could be the way it's going to be or it could have been a unique episode," the nurse said, typing into her laptop. "But I'll note this in his record so you can discuss it with his regular nurse when she comes later this morning." She looked up at the weary Tara and said firmly, "Don't be afraid to use the morphine. That's why it's there. It won't hurt him."

Cozzie was more or less back to normal when he awoke late morning, but he seemed to have lost something of himself. Tara caught herself beginning to mourn the loss of her uncle and wondered if losing him bit by bit was worse than losing him all at once. She soon learned, however, because after that night, the end came sooner than she expected. Within days, Cozzie was gone.

Day after day, Tara sat in his chair staring at nothing, thinking of nothing. At times, she wondered what she would do next. For the last seven years, she'd been a caregiver. First for her mom, then her dad, then her uncle. Before that, she had a boring but comfortable full-time position in the payroll department of a construction firm. She carefully managed her modest inheritance and worked part-time when the situation permitted. She didn't want to go back to her old job. Now, she felt purposeless.

Tara continued to attend church and signed up for new Bible studies. When she was out one day, she heard the pilgrimage commercial on the radio that she hadn't heard in months.

"There are still openings?" she said aloud and pulled over to write down the website and phone number given.

That evening, the plans were set. This pilgrimage to Rome would be Cozzie's gift to her. He left her more than enough money for it.

She arrived in Rome and wanted to experience it all. See life in the Roman streets, remember every detail of each church and artifact, and become almost an expert on the history of her faith. Her fellow pilgrims were fascinating people, many of whom had been on several trips and had experienced phenomenal events. Instead of dreading sharing dinner each night with a table full of strangers, she welcomed the opportunity to hear more stories of miracles. For Tara, the accounts hushed the din of countless other conversations throughout the dining hall.

"My husband and I went to Lourdes to pray for my cousin's healing," a woman from Michigan, whose name Tara could not remember, told the diners. "We prayed she would be healed of MS."

"Was she?" Tara asked, enthralled.

"No," the woman said with certainty, taking a sip of wine. She saw the perplexed look on Tara's face, anticipating the question: what was the miracle?

"She had a spiritual healing," she continued. "We didn't know until we attended the funeral that when she was diagnosed with MS, she became very bitter. She was so angry with God and thought God was punishing her. She felt like she didn't deserve an imprisonment like MS. Oh, my, how she suffered! Lost all her faculties. In the end she could do nothing for herself. It was like a prison for her. She was completely dependent on others for everything. She treated her care-givers horribly, as though they were complicit in this 'punishment.'"

"I don't understand," Tara put down her fork and leaned in. "How exactly was she healed?"

"After our return from Lourdes, God sent her a lovely caregiver. This dear woman had to be an angel. She lost her whole family—her husband and three children—in a car accident. Can you imagine such a tragedy? We met her at the funeral and she told us the whole story. She skipped joining them to enjoy a spa day with her friend. Talk about anger and bitterness! And survivor's guilt. She would have been with them were it not for her desire to have a 'me day.' She never blamed God; she blamed herself. Gradually, with a bereavement group and spiritual guidance, she learned to accept the loss and under-stand the suffering. It took years, she told us. Without that experience, she said she'd never have considered working as a caregiver. She had been a school administrator. She learned, through her suffering, how important it is to be at the precipice of ushering a soul from this life to the next. As she tended to my cousin over the next few months and told her story little by little, she could see her softening. Occasionally, she'd ask what prayers she said to get her through and eventually asked her to help her pray them. Then she asked to hold a rosary, then asked for a priest, then for the Eucharist. When she died, she was completely at peace."

Dinner conversation each night centered around more miracles from pilgrimages.

Kel, a burly, black-haired man with mountainous biceps, reported that his brother-in-law was out of work for 16 months, but after many disappointments, lost hope after 10 months and fell into a depression.

"While we were in Medjugorje, we prayed for him to find a job," he recounted, his voice growing softer. "As we were heading to the airport for the flight home, I had a text from my sister saying he was offered the job he had wanted so badly six months earlier. It seemed that it was offered initially to someone internally who turned around and found another position with a competitor."

"When I went to Medjugorje with a group from my church, we saw the spinning sun," another traveler chimed in. "And my priest's rosary turned to gold!" Tara laughed because she thought the lady would hop off her chair.

Tara listened, enthralled with the stories. Nothing this dramatic had happened to her or to anyone she knew before this trip.

Each evening, Tara heard more accounts of miracles from different pilgrimages. Most of them involved everyday suffering of ordinary people who were ill or endured catastrophic losses.

"These stories make me think God isn't some ivory tower manager," Tara joked during dessert one night.

A woman from Connecticut, whose lipstick remained meticulous even after eating, addressed her comment seriously and compassionately.

"Oh no, Honey. He is with us through it all. If we think he's distant from us, it's because we don't bother to see Him, feel Him, listen for Him."

The accounts from her fellow pilgrims probably resonated with her more than all the churches and museums they visited, despite their magnificence and beauty. They lived such a tightly packed schedule, rushing from one site to the next. Tara, while not wanting to eliminate any of it, still felt frustrated and a bit sad from having no time to absorb it all. Even being on a pilgrimage, sometimes it felt like the emphasis was more on the stops than on stopping.

Yeah, yeah, another mosaic. Yeah, yeah, another tapestry, Tara thought. *Without stopping to study and contemplate, it all just looks the same.*

At Saint Paul Outside the Walls, the tour director wandered over to her as the others explored the breezeways while she sat on the grass of the courtyard.

"How are you doing, Tara?" he asked.

"I'm good, Zach, thanks for asking." She was pleased that he singled her out for a talk. He sat down next to her.

"I noticed you've been kind of hanging back from the group. Aren't you enjoying the tour?"

"Oh no!" Tara exclaimed, concerned she had offended him. "No, it's great! I'm just trying to take it in. Everything is so rushed, and sometimes I just want to spend some time. Like this place. It looks so Mediterranean and peaceful that I don't think I'm in Rome. I just want to breathe it in. But every time I do, I miss something else. I'm so afraid of missing out and forgetting this experience. I guess I'm just trying to figure out where I fit…with this group…with God."

Zach smiled at her; he'd had this conversation many times before. "Tara, I've been taking people on pilgrimages for about fifteen years now. Some have come on two, three, or more tours with me, and I can tell you that each person is on their own spiritual journey. Everyone's on a quest. You may not start to process this trip until you're home and going through pictures. Try not to be so hard on yourself. This is 2000 years we're taking in here."

She straightened her legs and stretched forward, exhaling. "But everyone is so Catholic and experienced. I mean, they were raised praying and attending church as a family. They know which mysteries of the Rosary are recited on what day. They've experienced major miracles. They went to Catholic school. It feels like they have such a head start on me. I was raised in a Catholic family, but believe me, I didn't grow up like that. I was not a good, obedient, Catholic girl in any way."

Zach laughed. "Try being a mid-life convert like me, finding your way into that group. I know it's kind of intimidating. But you fit in. With us and Him."

Tara appreciated Zach's comforting words and that out of three busloads of people, he made time to talk to her. She thought he only did that with the VIPs.

After a whirlwind tour of the Vatican Museum and Sistine Chapel in the morning, the pilgrims filed into the Basilica of Santa Maria in Trastevere, wandering slowly, looking up, down, and around, trying to take in from a distance the medieval art and appreciating this particular Santa Maria, since it was one of the first Christian churches in Italy. Tara walked in front of the altar, which seemed under the protection of, yes, another mosaic dome.

"Another day, another dome," Tara said. They were instructed to find a seat while they waited for the "Vatican official" who was scheduled to address them.

She sat, quietly considering the spiritual and historic place, and thought about the previous days of the other landmarks they'd visited. She appreciated them all, but realized it was in a superficial way. She longed for a deeper connection. By this time, Tara no longer wanted to take in everything. It was impossible, sacred places filled with art and architecture, some dating to the 12th and 13th centuries and others to the 3rd century. But she wanted to take in something.

Lord, what would you have me learn today through this beauty? Please, give me something. Please don't let this experience disappear from me like a rock sinking to the bottom of a pond, she prayed.

The Vatican official arrived, an elderly, pleasant-looking priest who greeted them warmly. His English was very difficult to understand, and he knew it. But he was friendly, animated and used a lot of large gestures and they all laughed together even if they didn't understand. But he had something very important he wanted to get through to his audience, that was clear. He kept pointing upward.

To heaven? What he could mean, the pilgrims murmured among each other. With much coaxing, he convinced one of the women to stand next to him. They quieted down to listen more closely to his heavily-accented English. He put his arm around the shoulders of his reluctant assistant and kept motioning upward. He began gesturing even more fervently, emphasizing his arm around the fellow pilgrim. Tara followed the line of his arm, her eyes resting on the mosaic over-head: an image of Jesus with his arm around his mother's shoulders. She'd never seen their relationship expressed in that way. With his arm around Mary.

Whatever the speaker was saying faded out for Tara. Images from her past flashed before her, darting around her mind. Events that, years later, made her cringe when she thought of them. Occasions that made her wonder how and why she survived them. There she was, in her mind, 15 years old and lying to her mother about staying overnight at her girlfriend's when she was really going to her boyfriend's. She saw herself in college in a hotel room with a man whose name she didn't remember and wasn't sure if she knew then. Then late in her 20s, dabbling in the occult, studying tarot cards and giving readings. She found herself in her 30s participating in a channeling session and eager to hear the messages of the dead that were summoned.

Then she saw herself walking on the edge of a cliff, treating it like a tightrope she could master. Sometimes she'd get a little wobbly, then somehow pull herself together and walk straight. Sometimes her foot slipped coming close to losing her balance but managed to re-align. Then she looked to her left, the land side, the flat, safe, stable side of the edge. And there was Jesus, with his arm around her shoulders. She couldn't feel his hand until she saw that it was there, softly covering her shoulder. He was neither gripping nor pulling her. He was gently guiding her back.

"No, no, just a little this way," he appeared to say. "You don't want to go that far."

The applause of the group slapped her back to the presenter who blessed them and was whisked off. She sat there, stunned and dizzy. Tara's head was spinning and she only felt half-conscious.

She gazed upward at the dome, studying Jesus's arm around his mother's shoulders.

"Did the dome just drop on my head?" Tara said wearily. "It sure feels like it."

Then the revelation occurred to her: *That's why I never went over the edge. I didn't know it, but He was quietly alongside me the whole time, even when I was turning away from Him.*

The group had a few minutes to look around before boarding the bus to go back to the hotel, and Tara headed to the gift shop, hoping they sold a picture of the mosaic. She couldn't leave without one. She was afraid she would forget the image and never find it again. But there it was, a beautiful 4x6 postcard.

Back on the bus, she tried to tell some of her pilgrimage friends about the experience. They were all gathered around the woman who had been the priest's assistant during his presentation.

I know he was sent by the Vatican, but is he really that important? Tara wondered.

He was rather important, but that's not what the fuss was about. His helper wasn't just an average pilgrim. She was also on the tour in an official capacity for her job with a Catholic organization. Earlier that day, she had met the pope and had pictures to prove it. She had a captive audience eager to hear the story. It was exciting. Every person on the tour imagined meeting the pope, including Tara, and now one of them lived the dream. Tara was happy for her and wanted to hear all about it. But at that moment, she had her own thrilling story. She felt like she had just met Jesus.

Alone, she settled into her seat on the bus. She slid the postcard from the plastic bag and began a private and silent conversation with the man she'd been seeking without knowing it.

You really have been with me all the time, haven't you? And I have had miracles in my life. Surviving all those really bad paths. Taking care of my parents and uncle at the end of their lives. Witnessing Cozzie's devotion. The priest inviting me to church. Finding this trip. Today, the day the dome dropped on my head... Tara laughed to herself, knowing this was how she would always remember this day.

She glanced at the pilgrims lobbing questions to the lucky lady who had met the pope. Then her gaze turned back to the picture, and she snuggled down in the seat.

"It's okay," she said, smiling at the image. "It's always been the two of us anyway, hasn't it?"

KYRIE

Andrew Seddon

The first time I saw Meredith—the first time after her demise, that is—I was driving home on a dark, blustery winter's night when the wind was swirling fallen leaves in a sort of macabre dance before piling their corpses against the hedgerows. I'd stopped by the parish church, Saint Dunstan's on the Wold, as I frequently did, for a time of quiet reflection and prayer. It always soothed my spirit to sit alone in the sanctuary, the dimness broken only by the red light over the tabernacle, the stillness disturbed only by the occasional creak from the building's timbers, and tonight by the gusting wind.

The time, as it often did, slipped away from me, and when I finally rose from my knees and departed, night had fallen, the stars obscured by tattered moonlit clouds. A few wind-blown snowflakes flew past, and I shivered and pulled up the collar of my coat.

The headlamps of my car shot twin yellow beams along the deserted, winding road; indeed, but for the occasional lights of a cottage as I passed by, I might have been alone in the world, a solitary traveler passing through on a journey that had no beginning and no end. Hedgerows and dimly-glimpsed trees reared up and fell behind, no more than darker shadows in a world of shadows.

Shadows.

That was what my life had become since cancer had stolen Merry—she disliked my pet name for her, commenting once, "What am I, a Christmas tree?"—from me on the eve of our wedding. And so my life had become one of insubstantial, amorphous, shifting shadows with no glimmer or shaft of light to dispel the gloom.

And God... God was a shadow, too, for if He was there in the darkness, I couldn't find Him. Having grown up in a devout home, I'd always taken His existence for granted. Now I wasn't so sure. I wasn't even sure that I cared.

The miles passed, unnoticed; I had driven this stretch of road so many times that my conscious mind paid virtually no attention. Not to the turns and not, on this occasion, to the speed limit, either.

And so I almost didn't see her.

I had to look twice at the figure that suddenly appeared in the head-lights.

Surely it was only some local woman...

But no, it was Meredith! I would know her anywhere, daytime or night, sunshine or rain.

Meredith! Standing on the roadside, one arm half-raised as if enjoining me to slow down. My heart skipped.

My first instinct was to slam on the brakes. But some more rational part of my mind restrained me—the road, I knew, was slick; the car had already fishtailed once or twice, and to hit the brakes hard would send it into a skid. I'd probably been fortunate not to be wrapped around a tree already.

I applied the brakes gently, glancing in the rear-view mirror as I did so.

She was gone.

I sighed.

A waking hallucination. I'd had so many of them, seeing—or thinking that I saw—Meredith in a crowd, disappearing before I could make my way to her; or sitting in the church, only to find that it was someone who didn't resemble her at all but perhaps was wearing a dress similar to one she used to wear; or walking down the lane; standing in the queue at the chippy we used to frequent; or any of a dozen places.

I saw her everywhere and nowhere.

I was told this wasn't an uncommon phenomenon. That didn't make me feel any better.

Driving slower, now, prudence having reasserted itself, I turned a corner, and there she was again. This time, there could be no mistake. She stood in the middle of the road, arms extended in front of her, palms out.

Stop.

I swerved to avoid her, pulled onto the shoulder, switched off the ignition, opened the door, and nearly fell flat on my face.

Black ice.

It had rained lightly earlier and frozen.

More carefully, and holding onto the car for support, I straightened and looked around, taking a few cautious steps.

Meredith was gone.

Of course. Had I really expected otherwise?

Jon, I told myself, you are really losing it tonight.

I exhaled heavily and went to get back in the car. As I did so, I noticed skid marks on the grassy verge. I walked over to them. A car had gone over the edge and slid down the embankment. There it was below, dimly visible in the grayness. Invisible, though, from the road. The kind of place a car could sit for days or weeks before being discovered.

Slipping and sliding, I scrambled down to it. The front end had buried itself in a ditch at the foot of the embankment, which had arrested the car's momentum.

"Hello!" I called. "Are you all right?"

There was no response. Maybe the driver had gotten out and walked away. I hoped so, because the thought of finding a dead body made me shudder. I pulled my mobile phone from my pocket and turned on the flashlight. It was enough to see a form slumped over the steering wheel.

Dead or alive?

I wrenched the driver's side door open.

The figure moved and let out a low moan.

I gasped at the sight of a stubble-chinned face surrounded by lanky hair—a face I recognized instantly—and recoiled. "Wesley?" Leaning forward, I touched his shoulder. "Wesley? It's Jon."

Eyes opened, but didn't focus. Blood dripped from a gash on his forehead. "Jon?" he mumbled.

"Yes."

"C-cold. My legs... can't feel them."

I shrugged out of my jacket and laid it over him. His face was pale, skin icy-cold and clammy. He looked like death.

"Don't try to move. I'm going to call for help."

He reached out a shaking arm. "I don't want to die, Jon," Wesley whispered, taking me totally by surprise. "Don't let me die."

I hesitated only for a second before squeezing his hand.

"You're not going to die," I said with more assurance than I felt. What if he had internal injuries? A broken neck? Head trauma?

"I'm... I'm not ready..." he said in a fading whisper. "Don't leave me, please..."

"I won't," I told him, amazed at the irony. Here was a man who hated my guts asking—no, pleading—for my company.

I called the accident in, gave the details as best I could, and waited for the police and ambulance to arrive.

The chill breeze sent me into spasms of shivers, and I wished I had a spare coat or sweater in my car.

Wesley moaned from time to time. All I could do was squeeze his hand and tell him to hang in there. Hang in there. The man who wanted me dead. Wesley, who'd tormented my adolescent years, who'd created in me feelings of anger, resentment, jealousy, and yes, hatred. Someone whose permanent removal from earthly existence I would once have applauded.

What ridiculous luck that I, of all people, had been the one to find him. Wesley and I—and Meredith—went way back together. Both of us had had eyes for Meredith de'Ath—well, most of the boys did. Actually, all of them. Meredith—"It's pronounced 'Deeth,'" she would say for the thousandth's time, especially when Halloween rolled around—had appeared a goddess to us hormone-saturated youths who flocked around her like besotted acolytes. Meredith, with her long golden hair, her lissome figure, and blue eyes that could sparkle one moment, and shade into serious reflection the next. But Wesley had been the one who had pursued her the most vigorously, mercilessly shoving aside any and all rivals, including me, the scrawny, shy kid who preferred playing the piano to playing football or rugby.

Not that I didn't try, sometimes sitting near her in class or at lunch, carrying on a stammering conversation about nothing while attempting to muster the courage to ask her out for fish and chips or pizza.

At least until one day when Wesley cornered me outside, hoisted me by my collar against a tree, and told me in no uncertain terms how he would rearrange my anatomy into a very undesirable configuration if I dared to mess with "his girl."

And so I had for the most part watched enviously, despite the glances that Meredith threw my way from time to time; glances that implied that I should be more self-assertive and that my attention would not be unwelcome.

As we grew up, countless were the times Meredith rebuffed Wesley firmly but politely. And equally countless were the times that Wesley blamed me for those rejections, despite my protestations of innocence, cursing me out and threatening one day to blow my head off.

"You just wait," he'd say, pointing his finger at me as if shooting a gun, and laughing.

In time Wesley, however, went from being a mere bully to a fun-loving hooligan, a yob who drank too much, played around too much, and never made any use of the brains God had given him.

In short, he was not the type of person that would appeal to intelligent, devout Meredith in the slightest. We'd all gone through First Communion and Confirmation together, but that had marked the end of Wesley's church involvement, until many years later when first his father and then his mother died and he made perfunctory appearances at their funerals.

But well before then my family moved, my dad's job taking him first to Canada, then Australia, before finally returning to England, and to my regret, Meredith became only a pleasant memory, followed as the years passed by a series of relationships that went nowhere, girlfriends with whom I could not envision a future.

I went to university, studied music, embarked on a career as a reasonably successful composer for film and television, and finally, tiring of city life, succumbed to the call of the fondly-remembered landscape of my youth, and purchased a house amidst those gentle hills where I could work in peace.

And who did I see on my first Sunday back at the old parish but Meredith? Sitting alone.

Alone. It was inconceivable!

It was all I could do not to rush up to her and throw myself at her feet. As it was, I made the responses by rote, too distracted to concentrate. A sin, no doubt.

Afterwards, though...

It was as if we had never parted, and the years rolled away. But shy, retiring Johnny had matured into confident Jonathan Quick, and Meredith into an even more gorgeous woman.

Meredith's smile and the light in her eyes captured me at once.

"I always knew you'd come back one day," she said as we stood outside the church in the bright sunshine.

"Don't tell me that you waited for me?" I exclaimed.

She laughed, in that light way that accounted for her nickname. "Let's just say that no one else came along."

"You're not... I mean, surely there's someone." I could hardly believe my good fortune.

She held up her ringless left hand.

To cut a long story short, it didn't take more than a couple of months until a sparkly diamond graced that slender fourth finger.

Nor did it take long for me to bump into Wesley Crowder. News travels quickly in a small town.

"Heard you were back," he scowled, jamming his hands into the pockets of his jeans, his features twisted into an angry scowl. "And I heard about Meredith." He spat on the ground. "Bloody thief."

I was hard-pressed not to laugh in his face. "Nice to see you, too, Wesley. Come on, Meredith was never your type. I've been gone for fifteen years. You had plenty of time to win her heart."

He tensed.

I was ready in case he aimed a punch—indeed, perversely tempted to taunt him to give it his best shot. For I was no longer the scrawny youth of years past. Running, biking, and weight training had added muscle to my frame, while his body, evidencing a considerable beer-belly, had dissipation writ large on his flabby frame, and so he merely cursed me and stalked off.

Now, trapped in a wrecked car, his life slipping away, he turned eyes wide with fear towards me.

His lips moved, and I had to bend close to hear the words.

"Pray for me, Jon."

Tough, carefree Wesley, who had never given a thought for tomorrow, asking for prayer?

And from me? Who hadn't prayed since my pleas that Meredith be spared had gone unanswered? Who wasn't even sure anymore that there was anyone to pray to?

I recited the Our Father. It was the only thing I could think of.

Sirens and flashing lights on the top of the embankment signaled the arrival of the emergency personnel.

And Wesley was still alive.

I breathed a sigh of relief and stood aside to let the professionals take over.

The police officer who recorded my statement whistled and scratched his head as he surveyed the wreck while the paramedics and firefighters extracted Wesley and carted him away. "How on earth did you ever spot it? Nothing short of a miracle, if you ask me."

Credit the ghost of my dead fiancée, I thought, but instead said, "Just lucky, I guess."

"Lucky for him, the poor blighter."

Back home, after warming up with a hot shower and a cup of cocoa laced with peppermint schnapps, I went into my music room, sat down at the grand piano, and studied the pair of scores I'd been working on. One was a Requiem that I'd begun after Meredith died. I'd completed the Introit, but had become stuck on the Kyrie. Hardly an auspicious beginning. The other was a commission—the music for a romcom. Trite, but it flowed easily and I'd been making good progress. More importantly, it would pay well. I laid it aside.

I spread out the pages of the Requiem open to the unfinished Kyrie. I closed my eyes and brought to mind a vision of Meredith, Meredith smiling, caught in an impromptu moment when we were walking along a woodland trail, in an instant that captured her nature to perfection. I let my fingers drift along the keys…

…and there came the melody and harmony that had been eluding me.

Kyrie, eleison.

Christe, eleison.

Kyrie, eleison.

Lord, have mercy.

Christ, have mercy.

Lord, have mercy.

I committed the music to memory as I went, thankful for that skill. I could write it down later. For now, I wanted just to let it flow and develop, to express the heartache and longing of my soul.

I could almost feel Meredith's presence beside me, sitting on the piano bench as she had often done... inspiring me simply by being there... her hand on my shoulder... the gossamer-light touch of her golden hair brushing my neck...

Being there...

Where was she now? What was her reality? What did she see, feel, experience?

Had I really seen her, there on the road?

Meredith's goal in life had been to be an agent of mercy. And she had been, to so many people.

I was sorely in need of mercy.

As was Wesley Crowder.

Which of us, I pondered, needed it more?

I didn't need to—or perhaps I did—but I went to visit Wesley in hospital. As I walked along the gleaming white corridors, past doctors and nurses and other staff, who should I see but tall, slender Father Lawrence leaving Wesley's room, folding his stole and putting it into the pocket of his jacket?

"He's not—" I began, letting the sentence hang as I came up to him, but Father Lawrence shook his gray-streaked head.

"He's still with us," he said. "Though hardly out of the woods. The doctors I spoke to are cautiously optimistic."

"Meaning that it's still touch and go."

He inclined his head. "That would be my understanding. I heard that you're the one who found him."

"In a sense." I indicated his pocket and raised my eyebrows. "Did he ask to see you?"

Father nodded. "I only ever met him at his parents' funerals, and knew him otherwise only by reputation—meaning that I can't say that I ever expected him to return to the fold. That accident may be the best thing that could have happened to him."

"A strange grace," I mused.

"Sometimes calamities happen for a reason. To call the prodigal home."

"I hope it's for real," I said.

"God knows, and time will tell. But I believe it is." Father glanced at his watch. "Sorry to run, but I have an appointment."

"I'd like to come and chat with you," I said on the spur of the moment.

"Call me. And bring that new hymn tune you promised."

Hymn tune. Named Meredith. One of the parishioners had written words.

"Will do."

Wesley looked as though he'd lost a nine-round fight with a 500-pound silverback gorilla, his form swathed in bandages and wrapped in plastic tubing for oxygen and IVs. The usual assemblage of blinking and beeping machines and monitors designed to give the patient no rest surrounded him.

He opened swollen eyelids and raised a hand a few inches off the bed as I came into visual range.

His mouth twisted. "Jon. I owe all this to you, eh?"

I hesitated, not sure whether or not the remark was meant as an attempt at humor.

"Seriously," he continued, "the doctors say I wouldn't have lasted through the night if it hadn't been for you."

I pulled over a chair and sat down. "Better to be like this than the other, eh?"

"Why did you do it?" Wesley asked. "Why did you help Wesley-hates-your-guts-Crowder?"

It was Meredith, I wanted to say. Meredith was the one who really helped you. Meredith was the true hero.

"Because of Meredith," I said simply.

His eyes closed as if in pain. "Meredith never cared for me," he rasped.

"She did. She cared for everyone. Just not in the way you wanted." I took a deep breath. "When I saw you in that wrecked car…confound it, Wesley! I couldn't just leave you there. If I had…I could never face Meredith again."

"Do you think you will?"

The question caught me off-guard.

I just did, I thought. But I knew what he meant.

"I hope so," I whispered.

"Well, you might have been the best man, but in the end, neither of us won," he concluded.

"True," I sighed.

"Father Lawrence was just here," he said. "It's not a good feeling, Jon…to be staring death in the face and know that you're not ready. I was certain I was a goner…" His voice faded away, and his eyelids fluttered.

I made as if to leave.

He struggled to rise up on his elbows, gasping as he did so. "Can you forgive me?" His words arrested my movement. "I treated you very badly…for so many years…"

I blinked. Wesley, asking for forgiveness? I could never have imagined the day. Something in me revolted at the idea. And yet, could I refuse forgiveness to a possibly dying man? Or one that might yet live, for that matter?

Wesley had a wound that needed to be healed. And so, I realized, did I. Meredith, knowing me intimately as she did, had seen this, whereas I had been blind to my own condition. Because I had never forgiven Wesley, much less sought reconciliation. I had walled off the hurts and resentment and let them fester.

For an instant, I could almost sense Meredith standing there amidst the clutter of poles... See her giving a nod, a gentle smile...encouraging me to do the right thing—both for Wesley and myself.

"Yes, Wesley," I said, meaning it. "I forgive you."

"Thank you." He lay back, and this time his eyes closed, his breathing eased, and I departed quietly.

"Is it possible?" I asked Father Lawrence a couple of days later following confession while we were still speaking in strictest confidence. "Could I really have seen Meredith? Her spirit? Her ghost?"

He rubbed his chin. Then removed and wiped his glasses.

"There's no official church teaching on the subject," he said at last, replacing his glasses. "But yes, the possibility exists that God could allow the soul of a departed person to return for some reason. Saint Thomas Aquinas thought so. G.K. Chesterton admitted the possibility of ghosts. You recall Moses and Elijah appearing with Jesus, and the witch of Endor raising the spirit of the prophet Samuel for King Saul—necromancy, though, being a very different, and dangerous, proposition than a spirit appearing by the will of God."

He regarded me sternly. "One should not go in search of such things. And it behooves a person to make certain that what they're encountering isn't a counterfeit."

"I'm not a meddler in anything to do with the supernatural," I replied. "I was floored to see Meredith...and she was there on a mission of mercy, to save Wesley's soul...and mine, too."

"Well, then, thank God for allowing her to appear." He took off his glasses again and tapped the end of one arm on his teeth. "Perhaps— and this is only speculation, or a hunch on my part—there might be more to this than we realize."

"Meaning what?" I leaned forward.

He waved his glasses. "Perhaps you are being called to something…"

"Other than composing?"

"Not necessarily. But perhaps a complementary or additional vocation or mission." He gave a hesitant smile. "Just a thought, Jon."

"I'll keep an open mind."

An additional mission? What on earth could that possibly be, I wondered as I left Father Lawrence's office? Wasn't composing enough? Perhaps I should forget the lucrative but inane films and focus on sacred choral music?

I thought I heard a faint chuckle as I stepped out into the late morning sunshine.

"Merry?" Her name left my lips reflexively.

I shook my head, bemused by my reaction.

And yet…could this new reality—this new phase of my life— possibly involve seeing her again?

If so, I was all for it.

I headed home feeling curiously elated.

But once there, doubt niggled. Would the feeling last?

Or would it pass, ephemeral, leaving me desolate once more?

I clung to hope.

And that night, for the first time in forever, I prayed, believing that God would listen.

And the thought sprang to mind that perhaps, her earthly pilgrimage over, Meredith was now pursuing her pilgrimage to heaven on a different level. And since part of the bond of love was to help each other reach that goal, Meredith, bless her heart, by Divine mercy, was doing her best to get me there as well.

What kind of love was that? One that I was not worthy of.

"Thank you, Meredith," I whispered into the night.

And thank you, Lord.

I had taken the first steps on my pilgrimage, a pilgrimage that was only just beginning…

Kyrie eleison.

WAY STATIONS

Jane Lebak

"I'm not leaving. I'm her guardian angel."

The Purgatory angel inclines his head, unrattled by the anger that surprised even me. In a voice like a breeze, he says, "You're welcome to stay. Some guardians step away when their charges can't sense them. Either way, her soul is saved."

I'm clutching that soul against my armor. The last hours have been a tsunami of tension and fear, but I need to focus on that last word. Eleanor is saved.

The angel gestures that I release Eleanor's soul. I don't. He says, "We'll check in frequently in the beginning, less often after, but you can summon us always." He's so calm. My armor is hot with the friction in my heart. "You'll want to guide her, but the souls choose the best way to go."

I mutter, "She can't hear me anyhow."

The Purgatory minister rests a hand on my forearm. "You got her this far. You've done a wonderful job."

If I'd done a wonderful job, wouldn't Eleanor have gone straight to Heaven?

I release Eleanor, whose soul curls into an egg on the ground. The Purgatory minister perches on a bush.

Sitting on my heels, I scan the area. Scrub. Stillness. I dial out my vision, but we're the only two angels and one human in scanning distance. Purgatory must be massive. My squad never needed to come because demons don't fight over Purgatory. Everyone here is territory they lost.

Eleanor's soul coalesces into texture, then contours, then into a shape. She's used to having a physical body, so she unconsciously draws her soul into its imitation. Legs, arms, hair, a face. Clothing, too. A business suit. She's dressed for work.

My armor clinks as I follow her to her feet. I, too, am dressed for work.

Eleanor scans the landscape much as I did. I cup my wings around her while she sheds emotions I haven't dared let myself feel. Regret. Confusion. Relief because she'll get to Heaven, but also dismay at all that has to happen first.

Like all guardians, I was kept apart from her judgment. She met Jesus alone, creature and Creator, and He gave her back to me as that luminous package. While I cradled her against my breastplate, shaking, He instructed me to bring her here.

Not to the fiery part of Purgatory. Not to the worst area. Instead, we're on a scrub plain, Eleanor encased in silence. She can't sense the angels, and there are no other humans.

Trembling, she searches for a place to go.

The Purgatory minister nods. "Motion is good. Sometimes they get stuck." He vanishes, leaving me with the impression that he's available at my call.

The sun lies at the horizon. That's the direction Eleanor's facing, so toward it, she walks.

Most human-angel dyads communicate during the purification, with the angel helping grind off the edges roughened up by sin. Some lucky ones even instruct their charges in divine truths. Not me. As part of Eleanor's expiation, she can't sense me.

Several Purgatory ministers have checked in. One chatty angel said, "The sequestrations are the hardest cases, but I'm not seeing any danger signs. You'll find it difficult, though."

I replied, "She didn't hear me during her lifetime, either." Inside, though, I thought, Sequestrations?

I hadn't realized the Purgatory ministers had classifications and subclassifications. The minister replied to me, "But even then, you could influence and protect her."

Eleanor removes her jacket. Soon after, the business heels come off in favor of business casuals. It's not really clothing. She's just altering her appearance.

The sun hasn't risen. It won't. Time measures change, but here the only change is in the humans. Eleanor's funeral could be happening now, or maybe it was ten years ago. Eleanor is unchanged, and therefore, no time has passed.

My wings quiver as I drift through the unmoving air, releasing the tension of her final hour...the demons' last fight...her death...her judgment...and my fright while she met with either her Merciful Savior or her Just Judge. I wasn't sure. At the end, with broken armor and a sparking sword, I'd called my squad for help. They didn't leave even when we reached the Judgment Hall. I'd known Eleanor wasn't prepared. I'd thought I was.

She made it. My brothers-in-arms congratulated me on her election while my mind reeled. I don't know what Christ told her.

She needs finishing. Angel swords are forged from our souls, but human swords are forged from steel, in fire, then hammered into shape and laid in sand to harden. She's being forged. It takes so much time.

"Most of them travel," the first angel had said while I gaped at this sparse land. "They talk about a 'faith journey,' so by instinct, they move."

I don't know Eleanor's destination, other than Heaven, but she can't walk to Heaven. At some point, Christ will declare her sins expiated and come get her. How that expiation will happen, I'm not sure.

It's the humans' free will, again. The ministers answer my questions, but it always returns to, "God meets the soul in the way it allows Him."

The chatty one quipped: "The answers you want don't exist."

She goes by Almitas. Although most ministering angels speak as though they're de-escalating a hostage situation, Almitas is chirpy. She expounds about different types of souls and their styles of growth. "The humans who anticipated Purgatory as a mini Hell have a difficult adjustment. They wait for the fire to do the work. We have to convince them to release their assumptions and eliminate the spiritual blockages that stalled them out."

I ask, "How will Eleanor surmount her spiritual blockages?"

"Again, the answer you want doesn't exist." Her wings rise as she shrugs. "The Holy Spirit will identify them to her. Every time Eleanor recognizes one, she'll make amends with God, then move forward." Her brow creases. "You may find the landscape changes whenever she reaches a new point of growth."

Eleanor trudges forward. The sun provides little light, and I'm unable to brighten her footsteps. She leaks memories of her encounter with the risen Christ. It wasn't the Beatific Vision, of course, and she's restless because she would give anything to be back with Him. Whenever the restlessness peaks, she moves faster.

On a rock, Eleanor finds a bag with her name. As her fingers brush the fabric, I feel a rush of grace. Someone's prayed for her, perhaps many people, and it's bundled up as this way station in the wilderness. Inside are four bottles of water.

I can't tell who might be praying. Eleanor wasn't close to a lot of people, and most weren't religious. This might be from her funeral, but I'd have expected more.

Who would have attended? I never understood how Eleanor passed through life with so few companions. In the army, we depended on one another. When I got assigned to Eleanor, all my squad mates blessed her. A mere blastocyst had a line of benefactors around the block.

Likewise, her family's guardians formed a team. When she lived alone, the angels in the apartment building banded together. You had to do that. Demons could blacken the skies, so the guardians interlocked like a Roman Testudo formation, sharing advice and frustrations and needs. We prayed with and for one another. They relied on my soldiering skills.

Eleanor walked alone. She commuted to work, drafted reports in her office, ate lunch at her desk, and returned home to her dog. She stepped over the sleeping homeless. She phoned her sisters and nephews. She made friends when she wanted, and she made no enemies. Most of her life, though, it was her and a Pomeranian.

As Eleanor drinks the water, she struggles to pray. It's stiff because she thinks there should be a formula. By habit, I add my counterprayer, then present the combination toward God with my heart. I would love to show Eleanor how real prayer lowers your guards so you can encounter God in your soul even while you experience God as Other.

Carrying the backpack, she walks again. It's incongruous with her other clothing, but she alters nothing. "They get stuck in their assumptions," Almitas has said more than once. This must be how Eleanor idealizes herself: proper, and dressed for business.

In the low light, my armor glints.

Have weeks passed? Almitas says it's not worth keeping track. The distance Eleanor's covered should have resulted in a change of scenery, but it's all the same. Periodically, she encounters way stations. Usually they're water bottles, and she tucks those into the backpack.

The most recent one had apples. Shortly after, she altered her clothing to hiking gear from when her nephews went apple picking.

They'd climbed a small "mountain" (a glorified hill with a marked trail) and afterward filled baskets at an orchard.

At an outcropping, Eleanor withdraws an apple. Eating and drinking must be habitual. When she tires, she does one or the other, as if assuming they'll replenish her.

I say to Almitas, "Oddly, it seems to."

Almitas nods. "They're graces in understandable form. Eventually, the humans will be resurrected to their bodies, so they stay on script."

Eleanor finishes the apple but doesn't bury the core.

A moment after, strands of emotion crescendo from her. She's hearing insects. In this crepuscular world, chin tilted up and eyes closed, she attunes her senses to the ever-present sounds she's ignored. Surrounded by the beautiful cacophony of peeps and whirrs and croaks, she grieves for all the living things in the world she left behind. While still on earth, the sounds of these tiny creatures could have told her about the glory of God, only she'd treated them as something to avoid or to kill.

Now, though, she listens. She is here. They are here. God is here in the sound, and because her arid heart longs so hard for Him, the symphony is sweeter than her apple.

A cricket lands on the core. It saws its legs together, a whine grating into the twi-dark. It's the same keen as Eleanor's yearning heart.

The light intensifies. The setting sun was actually rising all along.

When Eleanor encounters a stream, she alters direction to follow its glinting ripples. Perhaps she half-remembers the truism that if you follow water, you'll reach civilization. She may be lonely. Alternatively, a stream means she won't have to depend on way station gifts.

I'm not sure that's an improvement.

Almitas is pleased. "Sometimes a person who was too dependent on the opinions of others gets sequestered so he can realize the person

God wanted him to be. God may be using the water to teach her independence."

To the contrary, Eleanor craved independence. At her worst moments, she even resented how her dogs depended on her.

She walks on the river rocks, changing her shoes to something flexible. It's cooler here, and she makes better time.

With daylight in her orange eyes, Almitas grips my hand. "Keep faith. God's leading her to Himself."

I pray, *I wish You'd tell me how she's supposed to get there. I wish I could guide her.*

Time has stalled again, the sun hanging at mid-morning. Dragonflies hover over the water but zip away when Eleanor nears. The water gurgles over the rocks, and again I feel Eleanor noticing its beauty. This attention is new. During hikes with her nephews, she was intent on reaching the top, taking a photo, and retreating to the trailhead.

A short waterfall splits around a boulder. In its spray she sits, eating the last of the apples. She hasn't encountered a way station for so long, and with despair clinging to her, she's searching the horizon in all directions. Which way is God? If she's chosen the wrong direction, is it possible to reach Him from here?

Of course it is, I reply. *God's a wingspan away wherever you go.* I chuckle. For Eleanor, it would be an arm's length. *It's not like you're walking to Him.*

She's treating it that way, though—and so, I guess, am I. In my mind, every step is a payment on the toll road she constructed with her sins.

I pray, *What sin is she expiating now?*

God replies, *Are sins the only things that need purging?*

I stand in the spray while Eleanor nibbles her last apple down to the core. As a soldier, my first thought is that we purge demonic infestations. I know she's not infested. Demons can't come here.

Eleanor experiments with extending her mind into the stream so the water can carry her thoughts down and forward. Her smile broadens at this new sensation, warming me. Next, she turns her attention to the waterfall spray, although that's harder.

Her mind lights up: one waterfall, but so many droplets. Water flowing, water moving, one continuity, everything working together. With pebbles and river rocks and sand grains, and one boulder, this stream is one, but it's many. Eleanor's life could have been like this, separate parts streaming from God and back toward God, a free gift free-flowing, each grace connected to everything else. She bypassed a million presents, unwrapped and unnoticed—so many of those taking the form of the people in her life. Souls who could have blessed her. Souls she could have blessed.

She's crying, but she's amazed, and she's absorbing the daylight as though it's God's love because, in a way, it is.

She should have a guardian angel. She's just realized that. But she doesn't, and now she thinks she never deserved one because she'd have shut that angel out just like everyone else.

I clutch her hard. *I'm here.*

We sit a long while, praying with the water.

The landscape changes. Lush, this wetland hums with greenery while the sun glories at high noon. Vines bend the trees. They're the killing type, with tendrils that curl sixty feet toward the light. They ignore the branches they climbed toward the sky until the tree dies, and then the vines crash to the ground where they die, too.

Where there are no trees, the vines spiral around themselves, living stems over tangles of the dead. Eleanor can't walk through the thicket walls. The thorns grip her clothing and snag her backpack.

She's trapped in the heat, no way forward, only a hard way back. *Almitas said you'd know which way to go,* I say uselessly. Eleanor tries to listen for beauty, but she hears only the wind. God is in the wind, and the wind is moving, so she hungers for movement. Instead, tears on her face, she's motionless among thorns.

"Almitas?"

She arrives with a puff of dismay.

"Please tell me you've seen this before."

Almitas swallows. "Would that make you feel more confident?" When I shudder, she adds, "No one stays in Purgatory forever."

I reply, "Forever's a long time."

Her brow furrows. "If she's stuck, there's something she needs to learn."

I knew that already. That's not an answer.

Every inch forward takes so much time. Forever may actually not be long enough unless there's a break in the thorns. Eleanor extends her senses into the forest, but as far as she can probe, it's all vines.

Insects call, but there's no symphony in their sound. She considers the multitude of leaves, but she takes no joy in thinking of God's creations working together for His glory, not when all God's creation seems to have interlocked as a series of twisted stems.

A dragonfly zooms overhead. Branches rustle, and Eleanor glimpses a mouse. It vanishes into the tangle of dead branches.

She lets off a burst of surprise.

A moment after, she's adjusting her form, shrinking until she's tinier than she's been since long before birth, then also shifting in shape. She's envisioning that mouse and its quick feet and its easy passage through the thorn bushes. Suddenly she's beneath the branches, a silvery-white mouse herself.

With a thrill, she runs.

Freed from the tangles, she glories in her smallness and avoids the thorns, leaps over the roots, and speeds beneath fallen trunks. I'm shocked by her joy in running. For the first time, she understands the gift of smallness. She's not carrying anything. She's released the strong, commanding person she thought she was. The thorns can't hurt her. When she crashes by one, it bounces off her fur.

She catches up to the mouse, and they run together. It takes far longer to cover ground at this size, but at least she's able to move.

The thickets end at a cliff. The stone offers no purchase, so the other mouse stops. Eleanor doesn't. In a flash, she changes again—still small, but this time with wings and feathers. She leaps off the cliff and lets the wind grab her.

This is terrifying. A human shouldn't fly. But I can't snatch her back.

Eleanor soars on an updraft. Again, she bursts with joy: She's letting the breath of God command her, and as this tiny bird, she can let Him hold her.

She circles back and dives for the mouse. I try not to cry out as she makes herself barely large enough to snatch it with her feet.

Brimming in her heart is gratitude. Gratitude for the music of insects and the connection of water, gratitude for her smallness and the lift of the air, but also the burn of all the help she never gave anyone else.

She can help this one. Now, if never again.

I calm the mouse so it won't struggle. With her wings braced, Eleanor plunges up through the clouds.

The atmosphere goes still and hot, forcing Eleanor to land. Gone are the vines and the breezes, replaced by drought-cracked ground. The shadows are at a slant.

Eleanor becomes Eleanor again, cupping the mouse in her palms. She's lost her backpack but retained her hiking clothes. She waits for the mouse to change, but it doesn't. She laughs at herself, then takes stock of the area.

As she walks, her shirt and pants grow a half dozen pockets. She tucks the mouse into one. "I have no idea where we're going, but at least we can move."

I haven't heard her voice since she died. The mouse climbs her shoulder, so she unknots her hair and lets him shelter from the sun. "I used to keep show-quality Pomeranians," she says, petting it. "Every night, I'd brush their hair." She laughs. "Since you're here, maybe that means there are dogs in Heaven, too."

Because he showed her an escape from the thicket, she names the mouse Compass. At a blackberry bush, she holds one out to him. "Is it safe to eat?" she asks, as though food poisoning were possible in Purgatory. The bush is heavy with fruit, and Compass gorges until he flops on his back with his belly distended. After they eat, she fills her pockets, then scoops him back up. "Come on, clever boy."

She creates more pockets the further they go, and even a hood he can sit in. "I couldn't do that with a Pomeranian," she adds, "although Frizzle was almost the right size."

At another point, she says, "God's a long way off, but at least I can bring you to Him, too."

Almitas is ecstatic. "She's talking!"

I reply, "I wish she were talking to God."

Almitas clenches her fists. "That will come. She's made so much progress."

Eleanor draws energy from what she's learned, but I'm exhausted. I'm used to the motion of soldiering, deploying wherever the spiritual combat is thickest, but we've been traveling in a state of continuous stand-down. Nothing will attack her, so there's nothing for me to do. Every time she's grown, it's been a response to God, not to me. I'm not useful.

We crest a hill, and there are people. Five of them.

Eleanor backs away. They haven't seen her.

She can make it on her own. I feel her thoughts: She'll make faster time on her own, traveling in a direction she chooses. Even before I reflexively try to bring to mind the things she's learned, though, she recalls them for herself: the symphony of insects and the wholeness of water and the freedom of smallness, and also the joy of traveling with her mouse.

She can make it on her own.

She doesn't have to.

Five human souls plus Eleanor travel together.

One of their guardians gestures to my armor. "You can take that off now."

I huff. "It's been a few thousand years. I'd feel awkward without it."

Another guardian quips, "Dmitri felt awkward without a cigarette in his hand, but here we are."

A third angel mutters, "We won't consider what felt comfortable for Xian."

I say, "But I'm not the one in Purgatory."

"Look around." The first angel snickers. "Traveling? Struggling? You most definitely are in Purgatory."

Their duration here ranges from months to a century. Xian's guardian says, "After they get moving, though, it's usually a handful of years."

The angel who teased me about my armor nudges my boot with his toe. "Enough time to disarm."

I won't. My squad's waiting for me.

The humans support one another as they walk, hugging or hand-holding. Compass often rides on Xian's shoulder. Eleanor walks alone, touching no one. All have shared their stories with Eleanor. She shares nothing.

Mid-travel, Almitas appears, hands Dmitri's guardian a paper bag, then vanishes. The angel passes Dmitri his gift.

Oh.

Eleanor shouldn't have had way stations. She should have had me.

Should have.

The bag contains pirozhki and blini, as well as water. It's suited to share, but Dmitri doesn't. None of them do. Those prayers are intended for them. He grows visibly stronger, then raises his canteen. "A toast to my grandson, who prays for me once a week."

Xian sighs. "It would have to be my great-great grandson." As another traveler hugs her, she whispers, "I spent a hundred years on a hill, stuck like a stone. I should have been more flexible."

Standing apart, but with her eyes on Dmitri's rapidly-draining water, Eleanor strokes Compass. "I wasn't flexible, either. I had a plan, and if things didn't fit, I never made room."

That's the most she's admitted so far.

Xian says, "I've apologized five hundred times to my guardian."

Eleanor shrugs. "I don't even have a guardian angel."

Dmitri looks right at me. "Of course you do."

They're aware of me? So far, it's been angels talking to angels, and people to people. If the humans talk with their guardians, they do it quietly. I hadn't realized they could sense other angels, nor that Eleanor wouldn't detect theirs.

I suppose she's lucky she can sense other humans. Maybe at the start, she was sequestered even from them.

With unfocused eyes, she looks where Dmitri is gesturing. "I figured it had left."

I hug her even though she can't feel me. Compass does, though, and moves up her shoulder to nuzzle my chin.

Xian holds her, and for the first time, Eleanor allows it.

Eleanor encounters a way station, an apple and two bottles of water.

Eleanor tucks one bottle and the apple into her pockets. The group waits while she drinks, but as travel resumes, Eleanor turns away from the setting sun.

With Compass riding her shoulder, Xian takes Eleanor's hand. "Are you feeling a pull?"

Don't separate yourself from them. That's what I want to urge. *You spent your whole life apart, but now you have a team. Why break away?*

Eleanor gestures toward a shadow near the horizon. "That way."

Dmitri points in the direction he was going. "My path is this way," and Xian agrees. Eleanor takes back Compass and buttons him into a pocket. As a pre-saint, Xian's not going to steal him, and Eleanor surely knows that. She must be worried Compass would choose to go.

Eleanor hugs them, one after the next. "I'm going to miss you."

She's never missed anyone.

The angels bless Eleanor as she follows her shadow across the ground. I bless the party of humans, then follow.

Loneliness shears off her with every step, and the water hasn't helped. Her heart is exposed in a way it wasn't during her highly-scripted lifetime. She wanted a dog and got a purebred. She secured the perfect career and a one-bedroom apartment and filled up a 401K according to plan. She fit her sister and nephews into the life she wanted, rather than building her world around the ones she loved.

She existed in a suit of armor. It created the shape of a life, but it was empty. Now, she's made friends and relied on others. Walking away unwillingly highlights everything she willfully set aside.

"I'm sorry." Is she speaking to me? "Thank you for staying. You didn't have to."

Whatever she learned from her companions wasn't enough to trigger a change in terrain. The ground remains cracked beneath her feet.

Although the humans travel, Heaven isn't a destination. The souls won't converge on a single point as if that's the gateway. Christ is the Gate. Wherever they go, they'll encounter God. It's only a matter of how they'll allow Him to encounter them.

Eleanor aims toward a rock that might be a way station. An angel she can't see stands beside it.

You didn't have to, Eleanor told me, still protecting herself. My help can't threaten her autonomy if she didn't ask for it. It's true, though. I could be battling demons and hearing reports from Almitas until the moment Eleanor gets de-sequestered. Why haven't I? I've missed my squad every day. I'm a soldier.

I am a soldier. But I'm also her guardian.

It's awkward shedding my boots and gauntlets. As Eleanor nears the rock, I recall my weapons back into my soul. My shield takes a while to dissolve, but finally all that's left is the breastplate emblazoned with my squad's sign. For now, I have no squad. There's no war, only the war Eleanor is fighting within Eleanor.

As her guardian, I can't fight because the enemy of the one I vowed to protect is herself. But I can support. I can follow. I can pray. I can love.

God asked me if sins were the only things that needed purging. They're not. As she travels, Eleanor's being purged of attitudes and ideas and assumptions. She's laid down hers, but I've been carrying mine.

The breastplate vanishes. I'm wearing hiking gear to match Eleanor's, finally her full companion.

We draw near, and only when the angel turns to me do I realize it's not a way station at all. That rock is a human soul.

Eleanor rushes forward with a cry, laying hands on it and trying to rouse it. The other guardian chokes out, "He's sequestered," and I can feel behind his words that it's been years, years of the sun baking the wilderness and the soul failing to uncoil.

She calls, "Angel, he's frozen like Xian! Do something!"

As I crouch behind her, the soul quivers under her hand. Compass runs down her arm and onto the ovoid form. I've got one hand clenched around Eleanor's while I hold the guardian's with the other. Eleanor's prayer joins ours, and now we're three.

She pulls the bottle from her pocket and pours water into her palm, then rubs her wet hands over the soul. Those were her graces, but she's spending them on a stranger. The soul loosens beneath her fingers, so she does it again, finally emptying all the water because wherever it touches, he takes shape.

The soul has limbs. At the head, indentations become eyes and a mouth. The moment hands form, Eleanor plucks up Compass and cups him into the stiff palm. "Pet him. He'll help you."

Stony fingers curl around the mouse.

She shakes the empty bottle. "Angel, he needs more." Another shake. "Please."

The guardian releases a burst of light like a rainbow, and in the next moment, brilliant hands pass Eleanor a second bottle. "Thank you," Eleanor says, rolling the human onto his side. "Let's get his mouth open."

The shining hands help position his head so Eleanor can trickle water past his lips.

I'm wide-eyed because those hands aren't an angel's. They're Christ's.

He winks at me.

Groaning, the man fights to return to formlessness, but Eleanor rubs his arm. "You have to wake up." She looks up, saying, "Can you—" and then stops when she sees Jesus.

Pleased, Jesus says, "What do you want me to do?"

The human soul starts to sob. Eleanor whispers, "I want You to help him."

The other guardian is on his knees, hands covering his face, crying. The soul is crying. And as I watch my charge and my God working together, I start crying, too.

It's dusk again.

Kurt, the human soul, sits with his guardian at his back, although he can sense neither me nor his guardian. He alternates stroking Compass with eating Eleanor's final apple.

He and Jesus have spoken at length. Kurt's been stuck for fifty years, but he's ready to begin his journey.

He rasps out, "Can Compass come with me?"

Eleanor's eyes shine as she passes Kurt the mouse. "He got me through a lot."

Jesus turns to her. "It's time to go." When Eleanor startles, He says, "You're ready."

She glances at Kurt. "Should I? Will he be okay?" When Jesus nods, she says, "And Xian? Can you redirect the rest of my care packages to her?"

Softly, I laugh, and she looks right at me. Recognizes me.

I clasp her as she buries herself in my wings. I say, "Did you really ask Jesus if you should stay in Purgatory?"

She tightens her grasp. "You didn't leave me."

"You both needed to learn." Jesus draws her to a stand. "Now, though, it's time to come home."

THE GLORIOUS PILGRIMAGE OF MARGARET HENDERSON

MaryJo Thayer

Veronica Milford's dying mother had survived her fifth coughing jag of the day, leaving her, as well as Veronica, exhausted. Both needed a break.

"I'll be in the living room, Mama."

"Mm-hm, Ronnie." She lay her turbaned head back onto her pillow and smiled sweetly.

"Would you be more comfortable without your turban?" Veronica asked.

Her mom smiled again and even managed a wink. "No, dear. I want to look my best for Jesus."

Classic Mama. Veronica smiled back at her, even though her mother's eyes were closed. Leaving the bedroom door cracked, just in case, Veronica returned to the kitchen. She turned on the flame under the tea kettle to finish making herself some chai—her third attempt of the day. She carried the hot drink into the living room and used an old *Reader's Digest* for a coaster, lest the ceramic cup leave a ring.

She slumped herself into one of the antique rosewood chairs, which were separated by a bulky-legged table that held the steaming tea, along with an ornate floral lamp and an icon of the Blessed Mother in an olivewood frame. Her mother had chosen it from a gift shop somewhere in the Holy Land—a stop on a pilgrimage that her parents had taken for their twenty-fifth wedding anniversary.

Veronica slid her hands back and forth over the rose velvet of the chair, observing the hues change depending on the direction of her swipe. It was a mindless activity, but one that distracted her long enough for her jaw to relax.

She couldn't get comfortable, even when she rested her feet on the small, upholstered ottoman that matched the chair. So, she picked up her chai, and ambled across the narrow living room to alight herself on a small sofa—one of those that had a high back on one end and no armrest on the other. She attempted to sip her tea, but it was scalding, and she burned her tongue. "Ow!"

She set her cup onto a copper coaster on the coffee table and picked up the neatly folded pastel tartan throw at the foot of the sofa. Her mother had selected it at the Celtic Craft Center in Edinburgh, Scotland, on a trip she took with Veronica's aunts after her dad died. Veronica spread the small blanket over her lap. She examined its light hues—blush, mint, silver, and ivory—the perfect choice for the Victorian motif of her childhood home. Leaning her head back against the high fabric corner, she took a long breath and exhaled. "Ah, much better."

What she really needed was a good nap, but she was too antsy about her mom to allow herself to doze. Veronica's greatest fear was missing the opportunity to minister to her mother in the final moments. The possibility of it made her throat tighten. She took out her cell to dial her husband, Christopher. After consideration, she put the phone back into the pocket of her hoodie. She did not want to overreact, and it wasn't likely her mom would pass tonight anyway. The hospice nurse who checked on her that morning assured Veronica that her mother's heart was still beating strongly.

She tried her tea again—now the perfect temperature. The chai tasted so deliciously spicy that she wanted to gulp it down, but she recalled her mother's adage about savoring the good things in life. She let the warmth sit in her mouth a few seconds before swallowing, as if to slow the passing of time. Veronica shut her eyes, as reminiscent thoughts rambled in her head.

Mom's a world-class savorer, that's for sure. Veronica recalled the many times her mother had made a peppermint candy last in her mouth for hours. "Like magic," Veronica mumbled. She rolled her eyes at talking out loud to herself, a habit she had acquired during the recent long days and nights at her mom's.

She had been on duty for the better part of two weeks. Her sisters had been wonderful in asking for time off work to share the load ever since their mother had entered palliative care, but none of them could swing even a night as of late. Veronica didn't mind. She's the one who lived nearby, and all her children were grown. It made sense for her to do the lion's share. It was bittersweet work that Veronica regarded as a privilege, and not just because their mother had been a peach to care for.

Margaret Henderson, or Mama Mags as she was affectionately called, had been a shining example of feminine genius—faithful, organized, empathetic, and calm—for as far back as Veronica could remember. Her mother's ability to stay level had been particularly helpful when Veronica and her four sisters were all teenagers at the same time. Five daughters, ages thirteen to eighteen. Veronica couldn't imagine it as a parent, even though she had somehow lived through it with her sisters.

Luckily for their father, his job took him out on a flight early Monday morning and back on Friday afternoon, so he missed most of the hormonal explosions. There was no other way to describe what went on, especially if they were cycling at the same time. *Oy vey!* Veronica laughed out loud just thinking about it.

Their father had been the one to go to for advice on sports, cars, colleges, and careers. Things that didn't require empathy. For everything else, the five daughters sought out their mother.

If Veronica was ever filled with self-doubt about her ability to be a good mother to her own six children, she called her mom for a pep talk—a solid dose of "Mama Mags' Magic," as the family had dubbed it. They even had a sweatshirt and coffee mug made with the moniker for their mom when she turned sixty. She loved them!

Their mother had a profound ability to see the bigger picture and parse out the real issue at hand. She used to say, "Life is but one pilgrimage after another. We must seek Christ in every moment, and we don't need to get on a plane to find Him."

Chatting with her mom about the tough stuff of life was one of the things Veronica would miss the most. After all, Mother had been a veritable rock after Chris and Veronica's youngest child was born blind.

Most of the family members didn't know what to do with David, whose eyes stared blankly back at them. They would quickly hand the baby back to Veronica and say, "I'm so sorry," or "This is tragic," or "I don't know how you do it." None of those statements were helpful, of course, no matter how well-intended they might have been. In those early days of learning how to parent a special-needs child, Veronica often found herself wanting to yell back, "I don't know how to do this!"

Vernonica's mom, however, was different from everyone else. She called the local university and the county health office to see if they knew of any programs for the blind. She went with Veronica and David to his initial appointments. Beyond praying daily for the inter-cession of Saint Lucy, patron saint of the blind, she operated as if David were as normal as her other grandchildren. She treated him the same as all the rest and expected him to pull his own weight.

She didn't even flinch when he broke one of her Noritake plates while trying to load the dishwasher one Christmas. "Oh well," she said, "one less dish to have to wash. Please clear the rest of the table, David."

Her reaction was the same the summer she paid him to help her weed the garden. When he pulled out her parsley and thyme instead of weeds, she remarked, "I never cared for the taste of those herbs anyway." Then she took a twenty-dollar bill out of the front pocket of her gardening apron and handed it to him for an honest day's work.

The two of them fell to the ground in laughter over the mistake, and without missing a beat, ten-year-old David deadpanned, "Good thing you didn't make me work in your dahlia garden." Veronica's mother's dahlias in a dozen different hues were the talk of the town.

Where Veronica was overprotective of David, going ahead of him to ensure that he didn't fall and hurt himself, her mother merely instructed him about what was coming up in his path. Like the time he was five and headed toward the basement steps. "You're headed for the basement, David, and you have about four feet left ahead of you. Remember, there are thirteen steps down to a cellar of solid cement, so make sure you count each stair."

Veronica had started to rise from her chair at the kitchen table to accompany him, but her mother gently put her hand on Veronica's thigh to hold her in place. "He can do this, Ronnie," she said. "You must let him try because it's the only way he'll learn."

Well, David lost count and tumbled down the last few steps and banged his head hard against the concrete, resulting in an award-winning goose egg. Veronica rushed to see if he was okay. David cocked his head to the one side and said, "At least I saved myself some time getting down here." The whole family cracked up over that one.

Veronica remembered David telling her one night a few years after that fall, "I love Grandma Mags. She teaches me from behind. She lets me take my own 'pilgrimages.'"

"What do you mean, David?"

"Everyone else makes a big deal out of my blindness. They rush ahead of me to try to save me from boo-boos. But Grandma Mags stays put. She believes in me and knows Jesus is with me even when I fall."

Veronica knew in her gut that David had learned from the best, growing both his faith and confidence in the process. He delighted in trying his hand at things his sighted siblings eschewed—like mastering punchlines of stupid jokes. He relished being the star of the show. To that end, Christopher went to the Home Depot for some two-by-fours, plywood, and long screws to make a raised stage in one corner of their basement. Henceforth, David began to hone his craft by emulating comedians like Ray Romano, Steve Harvey, and Weird Al Yankovic, using an old hairbrush as a microphone. And now, he was doing stand-up in New York City. Under his flashy, stage-worthy jacket, he wore a T-shirt of his own that said, "Product of Mama Mags' Magic." He used it as a prop for his opening bit.

Veronica's mom had wanted to encourage David's love of performing, so when he turned six, she bought him an upright piano— without asking his parents. At first, Veronica and Christopher weren't pleased because their home instantly turned into a veritable talent show with each of their half-dozen kids now wanting to take lessons. Thank goodness for Mrs. Richardson, who lived two streets over in the same subdivision. The kids could walk to their piano lessons, and Mrs. Richardson gave them a family discount. And now, Veronica and Christopher's home was filled with yuletide music every Christmas, and it was one of their greatest joys. If Veronica's mom had not bought that piano without getting their permission, they might never have discovered their children's musical ability to harmonize into their very own choir.

Sitting there alone now in her mother's decked-out Victorian living room, Veronica mulled over her mother's keen intuition on how to bring about the best of humanity. Margaret MacArthur Henderson was an encourager, and Veronica wondered how in the world she could possibly live without her.

Without warning, Veronica began to weep. She allowed herself to sit with her emotions for a while, employing the advice of her spiritual director. "Don't chase away your feelings over losing your mother. Sit with them, accept them, and stay present in your reality. Pray for holy resignation," Sister Colleen had told her.

Veronica cried for a little while longer, then blew her nose.

Once her mother died, Veronica would be expected to assume the role of matriarch, and she knew in her depths there was no way she could hold a candle to her mom—her poor, cancer-ridden, suffering mother, who still managed to greet each day with a smile and a blessing. No one, save a saint, could match that.

Veronica secretly hoped her mom would slip away quietly in the middle of the night. She wasn't keen on witnessing her mother's final breath. She had been at her father's bedside when he died, and it all seemed so final, like someone had slammed the lid on the stock pot of life. Mostly, though, she didn't want to witness a painful death. In fact, after the past two months of her mom's gut-wrenching agony, a sleep-filled, peaceful death for her mom was the only thing Veronica had prayed for.

"Oh goodness, how I will miss her." She wiped her eyes with the backs of her hands, determined not to let the moment turn into another sob fest. Rerouting to more positive thoughts, she was glad David had been able to visit last month.

From a semi-reclined position against the corner of the Victorian chaise, Veronica took mental note of each wall in the living room adorned with, among other things, nineteenth-century chattels. She fixed her eyes on the wall adorned with crosses, holy water fonts, icons, and rosaries from around the world. Mama Mags called it the "pilgrimage wall." Slowly, she allowed her eyes to wander from piece to piece, trying to remember where each had come from.

Ten years ago, their parents had embarked on a three-country European journey—part vacation, mostly pilgrimage to Italy, Spain, and Portugal. They had made a list of everyone in their family, including themselves. The two of them had traipsed around Europe to various churches with names connected to the patron saints of each family member. Veronica and the rest of them would learn of this via postcards that arrived one by one during their parents' absence. Their self-designed mission was to go to a church pertinent to each person, kneel in prayer, and bring that family member a blessed rosary. Also, at each holy site, Veronica's parents selected a piece of artwork for their home to commemorate the pilgrimage. Veronica shook her head in amazement. Such an act of pure love and faith.

She glanced around again at the various other accoutrements meticulously displayed throughout the brown brick bungalow. There were enough mementos that each family member would be able to select more than one keepsake after the funeral.

The only thing Veronica really wanted was the chest-high curio cabinet with the rounded glass that had come from the old country with her mother's grandmother. Veronica's grandma had inherited it as the oldest granddaughter, who in turn left it to her oldest grand-daughter—Margaret. It only made sense that Veronica should receive it next, and she was pretty sure her sisters knew that.

But she didn't have time to worry about that now. Her mother was coughing again.

Veronica shuddered every time her mom fell into another choking fit, thinking it might be her last. And then there was the horrible wheezing and gasping, indicating desperate attempts to get enough air to continue living. Veronica wrapped her arms around herself and prayed, "Lord, have mercy."

"Coming, Mama," she hollered, setting down her chai, now too cool to finish anyway. She used her hands to propel herself upward from the tufted cream-colored chaise and finger-combed her hair before padding barefoot across the enormous wool area rug. Vernonica often thought that it was too pretty to be walked on. She wondered if the thick carpet tapestry adorned with golden vines and mauve roses would be too heavy to hang on a wall.

As she made the turn down the hallway toward her mother's bedroom, she paused at the Limoges holy water font, just like she used to when she was a child on her way to bed. Her father had brought it back from one of his business trips to Paris. Mother was supposed to have gone with him, but Grandma Henderson canceled her offer to babysit us girls just three days before the flight.

Memories of being eight flooded in.

In her mind, she was wearing the flannel nightgown her Grandma MacArthur had made, straining to hear the conversation her parents were having behind closed doors. Her mom had been sorely disappointed in her mother-in-law, as her father had. They had stolen away to their bedroom at the end of the hall to have a not-so-quiet discussion. Her mother had been looking forward to the trip because it was going to include day pilgrimages to Lisieux and Domremy, as Therese and Joan of Arc were two of her mother's favorite saints. However, there was nothing to be done about it. No one else could babysit the girls on short notice. Veronica remembered her two parents emerging from their room as a united front, her mother smiling as if she did not have a care in the world, and that's the last time it was mentioned.

Even now, the whole thing made Veronica sad and a little miffed. *She'll never get to Paris.*

She resolutely dipped her fingers into the small font, hitting her nails on the dried-out sponge. She blessed herself anyway, making a mental note to hunt for the plastic jug of Lourdes water, so she could refill the font. A few years after their father's trip to Paris, he took their mother on a long weekend jaunt to visit the apparition site of Saint Bernadette. Grandma Henderson did, in fact, babysit that time. It seemed a consolation prize for the full France excursion, but was a compromise French excursion, as it was all their father could manage as his since his business was in the throes of a busy time that demanded his attention. Mama Mags had happily lugged home as many gallon containers of Holy Water as the airline would allow, so

Veronica knew there still had to be at least one of them somewhere in the house.

For their fiftieth anniversary, their father had planned to take their mother back to Rome, her favorite city in all the world, but his diagnosis of rapidly aggressive lung cancer left him dead two weeks after he finished his chemo treatments.

Veronica paused outside her mother's bedroom for a second, trying to muster up a peaceful countenance. Sighing, she pushed open the solid oak, six-panel door and made her way across the gray-blue Berber carpeting to her mother's bed.

Veronica grabbed a soft cloth and held it to her mother's mouth to catch her blood-tinged sputum. Damn lung cancer.

Her father had died from the same blasted stuff seven years ago when Mom was the healthiest that she had ever been. She herself had not smoked in nearly twenty years. She had also cut gluten and sugar from her diet and had even started lifting hand weights and going for long walks.

Doctor Langenburg had proclaimed her "healthy as a horse" and was still holding on to that last year when Mama Mags complained about numerous colds that didn't seem to want to go away. He would listen with his stethoscope and then simply prescribe her an antibiotic for bronchitis or pneumonia. It wasn't until Vernonica had insisted on going to her mother's appointment four months ago that the doctor agreed to run some tests. The results were conclusive: stage four lung cancer. *And now, here we are.*

Veronica took the soiled cloth into the en-suite half bath, washed it out in the sink, and laid it over the edge of the plastic hamper to dry. When she plodded back to the bedside, she found that her mom had tried to prop herself up but was tilting so far to the right that Veronica thought her mom might fall out of bed. As she reached under her mother's armpits to position her a little straighter, her mom wheezed, "A little morphine, please, Ronnie."

"Sure, Mom. Anything else you want?"

"One of those Magnum mini bars. Carmel, please, if there is one. Are there any caramel left?"

Veronica smiled, "I'll check." Her mother's two favorite indulgences had always been caramels and chocolates. If they came together, all the better. When Veronica had found the combination Magnum bars at the Kroger store, her mother had acted as if she had won the lottery, which pretty much summed up how Margaret Henderson felt about life.

Veronica came back to the bedroom with both the liquid morphine drops and the ice cream. She set the sweet treat on the intricately carved mahogany bedside table and unscrewed the cap of the medicine. "Here you go, Mama. Open a little wider, please." Veronica gently slid the dropper under her mother's tongue. She gave the bulb the tiniest squeeze and removed the dropper, placing it back in the bottle. Her mother closed her eyes and rested her head back against the headboard until the drug took effect.

When her mom was ready, she opened her eyes again and wiggled her eyebrows up and down in such a cute way that Veronica giggled.

"I am pretty darling, aren't I?" her mom asked with a raspy voice and a wink. Then she raised her hand up to her pink turban and said, "Who could resist me in this high fashion?"

Veronica shook her head in wonder. "Mom, I hope to be half the woman you are someday."

Her mother patted her hand on top of Vernonica's and said in a gravely twang, "You already are. Now, where's my ice cream?"

Veronica peeled off the wrapper and handed the small bar to her mother, whose crinkly, veiny hand reached out and tried to grip the stick. She was too weak to hang on, so Veronica held it to her mouth as her mom took slow, small nibbles. She only ate about a third of the tiny treat before whispering, "Enough."

Veronica grabbed a napkin and placed it under the melting confection before throwing it into the small trash can by the door next to the dresser.

Clear as a bell, Veronica's mom said, "Now go get one for your-self, Ronnie."

Veronica obeyed and came back with a vanilla one.

"Let's watch *Jeopardy*," her mom said.

And even though Veronica thought her mother should rest, she picked up the remote and pushed buttons until Alex Trebek's famous voice could be heard.

"He's got it worse than I do," her mother said as if it were a fact.

Although pancreatic cancer was known to be one of the worst and fastest advancing cancers, Veronica knew firsthand—twice—that lung cancer was no picnic. She had the urge to tell her mother that, but didn't.

"You know, Ronnie," her mom spoke in truncated, wheezy syllables, "life...is...short... But ...I—I've... had a... blessed... one. And...you have...as well." Her mom sighed as if energy had been drained out of her.

"I know, Mama."

"I hope you do, Ronnie."

Veronica patted her mom's hand and held it there. "I do, Mom. You rest now." Veronica lowered her head to look at their two hands resting together on top of the pastel peach velour blanket. One was thin and veiny with crooked fingers and age spots. The other, a little more youthful by comparison. On impulse, Veronica pulled her cellphone out of her pocket with her free hand and snapped a photo.

Her mother's recent comments caused Veronica to revisit her own life. She had met Christopher in college. After their wedding in the summer between their junior and senior years, they moved into married housing and welcomed their first child the day after graduation. Though they had their share of crosses to carry during their thirty-five years together, Veronica knew she had been blessed beyond measure, just as her mom had reminded her moments ago.

Vernonica offered a prayer of thanksgiving for everything she had, especially grateful for the opportunities God had given her to care for her mother.

In that instant, Vernonica ceased worrying about what was to come next. She had always had everything she needed. Nothing could change that going forward. Not even death.

Bittersweet tears escaped her eyes and trickled down her cheeks. Veronica quietly slipped her fingers from her mother's hand and found the nearest tissue before resuming her seat next to the bed.

Her mother continued to sit upright, pretending to be interested in the game show, but Veronica could hear soft, labored snores. Veronica glanced at her mother's peaceful countenance and smiled. It was as if Alex Trebek had lulled her to sleep. Veronica continued to watch, knowing full well that if she turned it off before the Final Jeopardy was completed, her mother would stir and make her rewind to the beginning.

When the show's music concluded, Veronica gave the power button on the remote a push. She closed the drapes on the windows and turned toward her mom, ready to help her settle down into a more comfortable sleeping position. It was then that Veronica realized her mother had already drifted off. For the last time.

Veronica gasped and her breath caught, but she didn't panic like she thought she was going to. Instead, she leaned over and kissed her mom's forehead. "It's okay, Mama. I'm so glad you're out of pain and with Dad. I know you've missed him." Then she thanked her mother for being the best role model ever and phoned each of her four sisters and the parish priest. Father Cunningham was there in no time.

Beatrice arrived forty-five minutes later, hugged Veronica a long time, and then headed straight to their mother's room. Amanda and Kathleen arrived together thirty minutes later. Veronica gave each of them time alone in the room so they could privately say everything they needed to. Dianna, being the farthest away, got there just before ten.

Eventually, the five of them rejoined at the bedside, holding rosaries from their parents' pilgrimage. The priest prayed all the appropriate and beautiful prayers and departed. The sisters knelt, and as they had done hundreds of times in their youth, they blessed themselves, kissed Jesus's feet on their crucifixes, and began to pray the Rosary.

Veronica knew that wherever her mother's soul was, all was as at it should be. Veronica's prayer for a peaceful death had been answered. Indeed, all was well, as if their mother had willed it so in her final moments before letting herself go to God. It was her last display of Mama Mags' Magic and her final pilgrimage. And it was glorious.

THE KING'S PILGRIMAGE

G. M. Baker

Men pushed the ship off the sand until it floated. The king kissed his wife and tousled the hair of his son. In each case, the gesture was fond rather than passionate. He took off his crown, worn today for the sake of this ceremony, and handed it to his steward. His robe and tunic followed, and the rings and brooches that he wore. Finally he let fall his trousers and stood shivering in his drawers. The bishop came forward and placed the pilgrim's robe over the king's head. The king let the rough, plain garment fall over his shoulders and down to his knees, leaving pale legs bare to the wind. He knelt before the bishop, who took a sharp knife, cut a circle of hair from the king's head, and sprinkled his bare head liberally with ashes. The bishop made a blessing over the king, and the king rose and, without looking again at his wife or son, strode out into the waves and boarded the ship.

It was a pale, blustery day, cool rather than cold, but the boy felt cold all the same. The sea had assumed a grey slate color, very like to the ashes on his father's head. All ornament had been stripped from the ship, and all its bright paint daubed over with black pitch. Even the sand seemed grey in the boy's eyes. Only one patch of color remained in the scene: the red dress that his mother wore, bright with gold and jewels, all she owned put on at once, it seemed, as if she meant to set herself in balance against the greyness of the whole world.

"Why does Papa go on pilgrimage?" the boy asked his mother.

"He has killed many men."

"Will I kill many men when I am king?" the boy asked flatly.

"It is the way of kings," his mother replied, her voice as flat as his.

"Will I have to go on pilgrimage then?"

"Would you like an apple?" his mother said.

"Yes, Mama," the boy replied.

"Let's go back to the hall," the queen said.

"I want to watch the ship sail away," the boy replied.

"Suit yourself," the queen said. "I may have eaten the apple myself if you stand here too long."

The queen turned and walked back to where the horses waited. The bishop and the retinue followed her. The boy remained, following the ship with his eyes as the wind took hold of the sail and drew it slowly out over the heaving grey ocean. It was almost an hour before he finally lost sight of the sail among the clouded haze of the horizon.

When he got back to the hall, he found the core of an apple waiting for him, browning and marked by his mother's fine, small teeth. He ate it and went to bed.

The boy was twelve years old, old enough to notice which of the young women of the hall, ladies and servants alike, were pretty and pleasing in their shape. Old enough to recognize that his mother was young and pretty, while his father was old and full of years. He was twelve, and his mother was seven and twenty, and it was small reckoning to know that she had been but fourteen and his father past forty when he had married her and taken her to his bed.

The boy had a half-sister, a woman past thirty. She would talk often of the great love there had been between her mother and the king. It had been a marriage of equals, she would say. Her mother, his first queen, had been ever in the king's council, and they had laughed together and loved and joked and sang. They had seldom been out of each other's company, and there had been light in their faces whenever they came together, even after the briefest of partings. She would talk rapturously of those times, of blessed days spent with her doting parents in the fullness of their youth. And when she was at last unburdened of these reminiscences, the boy's mother would say between gritted teeth, "But I gave him a son."

It was a fancy of the king that his queen and his daughter, being in his eyes of like age and custom, should love like sisters. At his wish, they were often confined to each other's company. The bitterest of sisters they became because of it, until his mother came to despise her own son because he was not his father's favorite child. The boy satisfied a need in his father. One need and one need only. His half-sister, however, was rather fond of the boy, which only deepened his mother's disdain for him.

"Why did my father have to go on pilgrimage?" he asked his half-sister over the game board one morning about a month after his father's departure.

"To atone for his sins," his half-sister answered.

"What sins?" the boy asked. All his own sins seemed to be public knowledge, proclaimed by his mother, who had a wondrous eye for sin, so why should his father's sins be unknown to him?

"Taking little tarts to his bed," his half-sister answered.

The boy colored because he thought that she meant his mother. But then he followed her eyes and looked upon the young kitchen slave whose face and figure had recently begun to invade his thoughts and occasion sins that he was terrified his mother would discover and announce. The girl was gathering rushes from the floor and throwing them onto the fire. A barrow of fresh rushes stood ready for her to distribute after she had swept the floor clean. She seemed rather thicker around the waist than when he had last made a detailed observation of her form. A pang of fierce resentment shot through his body.

"Do you want a brother or a sister?" his half-sister asked.

Another month and it was high summer. The boy toiled in the dusty practice yard with the other boys, watched and instructed by the castellan. His practice partner slipped and fell. The butt of his staff hit the ground and bounced up, striking the boy by his right ear. His blood up, he fell on the other boy and pummeled his head with his fists. Not daring to strike back against the king's son, the other boy covered his head with his arms as best he could until the castellan pulled the boy off him.

"Enough," the castellan said, holding the boy by the collar. The other boy got up slowly, feeling his face for blood and bruises. The castellan paid no attention to him but led the boy away to look at the scrape that the rebounding staff had made on his temple.

"My mother says that my father had to go on pilgrimage because he killed many men," the boy said.

"I do not think your father ever killed a man himself," the castellan said. "But many men have been killed by his command."

"Have you killed a man?" the boy asked.

"One," the castellan said. "Perhaps two. I did not see if that man survived the wound I gave him."

"Only two?" the boy said, disappointed.

"Battle is not what you think it is," the castellan said. "If every warrior had killed a dozen men, there would be no men left on earth. It is mostly pushing and shoving. A cut here, a bruise there, a cracked head. If a man keeps his place and remembers his instruction, he is not too likely to die. But men grow weary in the fight. If their captain sees that they are weary and has them withdraw in order, the battle is lost, but most men will live and return to their homes. But if there is no withdrawal and they grow too weary to fight on, they break. Then there is killing. Then there is all the killing a man can put his spear to if he has the lust for it. Or if a town falls to a siege. There is much killing then."

"If you have killed, don't you need to go on a pilgrimage like my father?"

"Someone has to stay behind to guard the land."

"So my father will be shriven and go to Heaven, and you will guard the land and go to Hell?"

"I have only done what the King, my rightful ruler, has ordered me to do."

"Did you like it?"

"Did you like it when you beat that boy?"

It was late summer, and the mornings were beginning to be crisp. The boy decided to go riding, but when he went to the stable, he found his mother there, her cheeks bright and straw in her hair.

"I've been riding," his mother said brusquely, though he had not asked.

"It's early, Mother," the boy said, puzzled.

"You're a slugabed," she answered snappishly and hurried away from him, back toward the hall.

"I didn't know my mother went riding so early," he said to the groom.

The groom grinned. "She likes a gallop in the morning," he said.

The boy perceived that he was being made game of. His mother's favorite mare was dozing in her stall. The mare had clearly not been galloped this morning.

"My father cannot ride on his pilgrimage," he said. "He told me that he has to walk the whole way."

"I reckon he'll have a trot now and then if he fancies one," the groom said. His cheeks too were bright like the queen's.

The boy rode to the bishop's house. The bishop came out to see him, complaining at being interrupted in his prayers. The bishop was an old man with a florid face and a fringe of white hair.

"Why has my father been gone so long on his pilgrimage?" the boy asked.

"It is a long way to Santiago," the bishop replied. "He must walk through France, cross the Pyrenees, and walk all across Castile and Leon."

"Will he be back before winter?" the boy asked.

"I expect he will winter in Spain and take ship in the spring. He would be a fool to chance the Atlantic in winter."

"I wish I had gone with him," the boy said.

"A hard road for a boy," the bishop said.

"I am hardy," the boy replied. He knew in his heart that his father would not have wanted so much of his company.

"Why did you make my father go on a pilgrimage?" the boy asked.

"He took land from the church to pay his debts," the bishop replied.

"Will you make me go on a pilgrimage one day?"

"It will be my successor who will have charge of your soul when you are king," the bishop replied. "Or my successor's successor. He will take measure of your sins and give you the penance that they merit."

"If you have charge of my father's soul, why did you not go with him on the pilgrimage?" the boy asked.

"I am an old man. My knees are weak and my sins are few. Besides, I have other souls to care for."

He mentioned his odd encounter with his mother to his half-sister. She laughed at his simplicity. "Do you want a brother or a sister?" she asked him.

Still he did not understand.

"We could soon have a fine young horseman in the family," his sister continued.

"But I ride very well," the boy complained.

"So does your mother," his sister said. "I hope no one will be cruel enough to tell our father of this when he returns. But if she crops, she will have to hope that he cannot tell a three-month child from a newborn. Oh, but can I live with my conscience if I become complicit in such a deception? Which would be the greater sin, do you think: to speak or to remain silent?"

The boy understood now. He stared at his sister blank-faced. The infidelity of men he understood. The infidelity of women was something he had never suspected.

"Have you ever…" he began but trailed off, cheeks flushed.

"Gone riding in the morning?" she asked him, amused. "There is no horse in our stables worth the trouble of saddling."

"Why don't you have a husband?" he asked.

"There is no man worthy of me," she replied. He could not fathom the peculiar, faraway voice with which she said this.

"Will you tell my father that my mother goes riding in the morning?" the boy asked.

"Do you want to keep her?" his half-sister asked. "I'd as soon see her gone. But if you are attached to her, I will see if my conscience will permit me to lie to our father for your sake."

Another month went by. A man in pilgrim garb passed through the town. He was thin as twigs. His hair was long and knotted and shot with grey. His face was creased and blotched and looked like old leather. His feet were bare and his legs were grimed with the dust of the road up to his knee. The boy saw him pass and wondered if his father now looked the same, wherever he might be on the road to Santiago. He ran after the man and asked him to stop and talk to him.

"Why are you on a pilgrimage?" the boy asked. "What sin did you commit?"

"It was no sin of mine," the emaciated man said. "The bishop pays me to make reparation for his sins so that when he dies he will go straight to heaven."

"I did not know that you could make reparations for another person's sins," the boy said.

"It is how I manage to feed my wife and children, though I have broken hands and cannot work," the man said. He showed the boy his hands, which had been crushed by a barrel that had fallen and broken his knuckles, which, as he showed the boy, he could barely move.

"Then why did my father have to go on pilgrimage for himself?" the boy asked. "He has many men he could have sent to make a pilgrimage for his sins. He could have stayed at home, and my mother would not have needed to go riding in the early morning."

"I cannot answer that, master," the man said. "But I am grateful to bear the bishop's sins, for they put bread in the mouths of my children."

"Are you going to Santiago?" the boy asked.

"Oh, that is too far for me," the broken pilgrim answered. "I go to the Shrine of the Saint. It is but seven days from here. I know the road well, for I walk it once in each season of the year."

"Can you tell me how to find this road and this shrine?" the boy asked.

"I want to go on a pilgrimage," the boy said.

"Why, what sin have you committed?" his mother asked. She put her hand over her mouth as if she were trying to hold in a belch. She had seemed nauseous every morning for the last week.

The boy thought about the lust he felt for the young kitchen slave, the strange pleasure he had taken in feeling his fists pummel his training partner's head and the satisfaction he had felt in seeing the cuts and bruises his fists had left on the boy's face.

"I want to make reparation for my father's sins," he said, "so that he can come back to us sooner."

"Your father is in Castile or Leon," she replied. "He is a guest of the king, drinking rich red wine and taking pretty Moorish slave girls to his bed. How would he know that you had made reparation for his sins? And what makes you think you can make reparation enough for all the new sins he is committing? He will come back when it suits him, his soul as black as on the day he left."

"I don't believe you," the boy said. He knew his mother to be a sinner, and he did not trust her word. "I will make reparation for his sins. He will feel his soul grow light within him, and he will come hurrying back and embrace me as his son and heir."

"Well, you can't go," his mother said. "You are his heir. If you died he would send me away and there would be no one to look after me when I am old."

The boy wanted to say, "Let the bastard in your womb look after you," but the words seemed too impious for his tongue.

"I know the road," the castellan said. "It is a hard and stony way, set about with thorns. But there's not much danger on it. Pilgrims do not carry enough to make it worth a bandit's while to haunt that way. A good soldier who knows his business should have no trouble on that road."

"Will you come with me, then, so that I do not offend my mother by getting killed?" the boy asked.

"Come as a guard or as a pilgrim?" the castellan asked.

"That you must choose for yourself," the boy answered. "I walk for my father's sins, not my own," he added.

"I could do that," the castellan said.

The boy and the castellan walked through the town. They wore only pilgrims' tunics, and their legs were bare to the knee. They had cut their hair and covered their heads with ashes. The boy went barefoot, though the castellan had shoes on his feet. The castellan carried a staff and had a sword and dagger belted around his waist, the necessities of his office. The boy carried no staff or weapon.

They passed the bishop's house. A curate carried word of their coming to the bishop, who left his prayers to hurry out and meet them on the road. He admonished them for beginning a pilgrimage without leave or payment.

The boy said, "I have a gift for the shrine, but I did not know I was supposed to have one for you also."

"It has been the custom since time immemorial," the bishop said.

"I will know that next time," the boy said, and he and the castellan walked on. The bishop went back angrily to his prayers.

News of the boy's pilgrimage was carried back to the hall and reached his mother's ears. She ordered her horse to be saddled and rode after him with an escort of twenty men. His half-sister heard the commotion and had her own horse saddled so that she would not miss any of the scene between mother and son.

It took two days for the queen's party to catch up to them, for it had taken a long time to load carts with food and other comforts of a journey. At the end of that day, the boy and the castellan stopped to beg for their supper from a peasant farmer. Coming out of his house, the farmer was astonished to see that a royal encampment with tents and braziers and twenty horses at least was setting up in his fallow field. Since the field was fallow, the farmer made no objection. Twenty horses meant a lot of free manure. He was too polite to ask why the two mendicants did not go begging to the royal camp instead of coming to his door, where he had only the most plain fare to offer them. He fed the boy and the castellan on pottage and hard black bread and allowed them to sleep in a hayrick.

In the morning, the queen, though she was feeling particularly bilious that morning, sent a herald to summon the boy and the castellan into her presence.

"There's a good breakfast making," the herald said by way of inducement. "She'll eat none of it," he added knowingly.

"Mind your manners, soldier," the castellan said. "Deliver your message."

"I'm to tell you to come and tell you if you don't, she'll send men to fetch you."

"She knows I am the captain of those men?" the castellan said.

"I couldn't say, sir," the herald said. "She's..." He trailed off, remembering his captain's former admonition.

"We should go," the boy said. "It would be prideful not to. But I'm not going back to the hall."

"Right then," the castellan said.

"I don't want to make trouble for you, though," the boy said.

"She's in no position to make trouble for anyone," the castellan replied. The herald sniggered, and the castellan froze him with a look.

There was a table laid with plates of fat sausages, pink juicy bacon, glistening fried bread, shiny boiled eggs, and crisp fried potatoes. Jars of ale, wine, and buttermilk stood ready to be poured. At one end of the table the queen sat, endeavoring not to look at the table or allow any of its aromas to reach her nostrils. At the other end sat the boy's half-sister, tucking into a large platter of eggs, sausages, and fried bread and washing it down with a large mug of beer. Between bites, which she masticated loudly, she paused to praise the rich flavors and aromas of the sumptuous meal and to encourage the queen to take a plateful and tuck in.

The half-sister put down her knife and grew silent when she saw the castellan in his pilgrim garb with the unwashed stain of ashes on his head and cheeks. At fifteen, her father had discovered her passionately kissing a young squire behind the stables. The castellan still bore the stripes on his back from the whipping he took that day. She, furiously, had refused the suit of every knight and prince for five years, and after that, though she had grown out of the years of passion and into the years of foresight, the habit had become so ingrained in her and her intransigence had become so well known that a maid she had remained. He had grown hard and she bitter. She saw him again in that moment as she had seen him in his youth, with all his pride stripped away. She rose from the table and hurried away, not looking back though she knew that the eyes of the castellan followed her.

"You asked for me, Mother," the boy said. "How can I serve you?"

"Stop this foolishness," his mother said.

"I walk for the remission of my father's sins," the boy said. "I do not think it foolish to do so."

"If you don't come back with me, I shall have these men seize you and carry you back."

"Lady," the castellan said. "I am the captain of these men. It would be uncharitable to force them to choose whose orders they will obey. But you should have no doubt about whose orders that would be."

"Seize them," the queen cried in fury, rising from the table. As she rose, the boy saw that his mother was suddenly sporting a round belly like a woman carrying an eighth-month child. Not one man moved to obey her.

"Won't you put on pilgrim garb and come with us, Mother?" the boy asked.

"Can't you see I am great with your father's child?" the queen said. "How can you abuse me by suggesting such a trial in my condition?"

"Today I will walk for your sins, Mother," the boy said.

"Seize them," the queen cried, turning with fury to the armed men of her retinue.

Several men laid down their arms and began to walk toward the boy and the castellan, clearly meaning to join their party. The castellan waved them back to their positions.

"Take my mother back to the hall," the boy said. "For my sake, do not make game of her."

As they turned to resume their journey, the boy's half-sister came hurrying to join them. She had traded her fine dress and jewels to the farmer's wife for a grubby old working smock. She had cut off her hair with the farmer's shearing scissors and scooped up cool ashes from the edge of the kitchen fire to heap on her head. When she came up to them, she looked down at her feet. She stooped and took off her fine shoes and threw them into the farmyard. The castellan looked at his own feet, then bent and threw his shoes away in imitation of the one he loved.

They walked five more days over hard and rocky roads beset with thorns, and their feet were bruised and their limbs weary when at last they came in sight of the Shrine of the Saint. When he saw it, the boy fell on his knees and walked the rest of the way on his knees. His sister and the castellan looked at each other and then knelt down and followed the boy's example. Slowly they approached the shrine on bloody knees. When they came to it at last, the priest who was in charge of the place came out and received their gifts. He blessed them and heard their confessions and gave them absolution, then said the Holy Mass for them, and despite their hunger and their bruises, they were filled with a joy they could not express.

They stayed several days at the Shrine of the Saint, resting and allowing their cuts and bruises to heal. On the third day a messenger came galloping from the hall. He fell on his knees before the boy and said, "Sire, I bring news of your father." Being addressed so, the boy knew already the news that was brought to him. His father had died, and he was king.

His father, the boy learned, had walked across France without let or luxury, garbed as he had been on his day of departure. The guides reported that he had been the most saintly pilgrim they had ever known, fasting constantly and walking barefoot over the roughest roads and through the thickest thorns. By the time he had reached a small shrine in the high wild lands of the Pyrenees, he had been worn to a thing of bones, and a cut in his foot had festered and would not heal. The priest who kept that shrine had heard his confession and given him absolution and viaticum, and he had died that hour, shriven of all his sins.

The boy ordered the groom to marry his widowed mother so that she should have a father for her child and someone to look after her when she grew old. He gave permission for his half-sister to marry the castellan and endowed them with a rich estate. He freed the young kitchen slave and provided a dowry so that she could marry the black-smith's apprentice who was sweet enough on her to consent to raise another man's child. Whose child he was raising he did not know and was never told. The boy who had been beaten about the head on the practice ground found a bejeweled dagger lying on his bed one day, though he never learned the source or motive for the gift.

As a king, the boy was of the middling kind. His name is not often spoken, and the chronicles record no great deeds from his reign. However, every year on the annum of his father's death he would put off his crown and his rich robes, don a pilgrim's garb, put ashes on his head, pay the bishop according to immemorial custom, and walk bare-foot to the Shrine of the Saint in the company of any who cared to walk with him.

ABOUT THE AUTHORS

G. M. Baker, "The King's Pilgrimage"

G. M. Baker lives in Nova Scotia with his wife, no dogs, no horses, and no chickens. He writes about kind abbesses and melancholy kings, about elf maidens and ship wreckers and shy falconers, about great beauties and their plain sisters, about sinners and saints and ordinary eccentrics. In his newsletter "Stories All the Way Down," he discusses history, literature, the nature of story, and how not to market a novel. You can find him at https://gmbaker.net.

Nancy Bechel, "A Pilgrim's Romance"

Nancy Bechel is a writer, editor, and book coach with a passion for story and a special fondness for bacon and chopsticks—and eating bacon with chopsticks. As a former youth minister and middle school teacher, she has a deep love for sharing the beauty and depth of the Catholic Church with young people, and drawing readers of all ages into communion with Christ through stories of all kinds—especially fantasy, adventure, mystery, and romance. Find her at www.WhenceTheAdventure.com

Karina Fabian, "Pilgrimage to L5"

Karina Fabian writes science fiction and fantasy and does stand-up comedy. She's the current President of the Catholic Writers Guild. She's the wife of a bona-fide rocket scientist, mother of four adult children and caretaker of two aging, demented dogs. She has no free time. https://fabianspace.com

Jane Lebak, "Way Stations"

Jane Lebak writes books and knits socks. Both are warm. You cannot have the socks. https://janelebak.com/

Mary McWilliams, "The Day the Dome Dropped on My Head"

Mary McWilliams writes stories centered around introspective characters and their pivotal, Jesus-led, "Come, follow me" moments, welcoming the ordinary to find the extraordinary—the "why" behind protagonists' actions. She is an editor and columnist for the Catholic Writers Guild where she pursues a variety of genres including book reviews, inspirational pieces and historical perspectives.

Karen Meyer, "Gold in Them Hills"

Karen Meyer was born and raised on the Canadian prairies, where small town life in a large family provided ample fuel for her imagination. Her short fiction has been further inspired by her travels throughout Canada and the United States. She and her husband reside near their three grown children in Ottawa, Ontario.

Rietta Parker, "Not All Who Wander"

Rietta Parker holds a BS in secondary English education and an MA in English-Creative Writing from Auburn University. She writes fiction, poetry, reflections, and prayers. When she isn't teaching or writing, she loves to sing, dance, and act. Learn more about her at https://riettaparker.com/home/

John Ruberto, "Faithful Journeys, Hidden Sanctuaries"

John Ruberto, a historical fiction writer and avid fly-fisherman, lives in Southwest Florida with his wife, Laura. They both enjoy going on pilgrimages and chronicle their adventures on their blog, https://hallowedway.com/.

Laura Ruberto, "Pilgrim in Name Only"

When she is not on a long walking pilgrimage with her husband, Laura Ruberto enjoys her vocation as a Vincentian, handcrafting one-of-a-kind greeting cards, and roaming the beautiful beaches of her southwest Florida home. https://hallowedway.com/

Andrew Seddon, "Kyrie"

The author of 17 books and many articles and short stories, Andrew M. Seddon writes science-, supernatural-, historical-, and non-fiction. A member of CWG, SFWA and the Authors' Guild, he loves travel and running marathons. Recent publications include two volumes of short stories about German Shepherds to benefit rescue organizations (*Bonds of Affection* and *Ranger's First Call*) and *Wolf Wanderings* to benefit conservation groups. He lives in Florida with his wife Olivia and German Shepherds Baltasar and Zara. His Author's Guild website is www.andrewmseddon.com

Judy D'Ammasso Tarbox, "Old Coffee Pots and New Beginnings"

Judy's writing journey began while still in grammar school with "The Exploding Chicken Noodle Soup," a humorous story about a cafeteria mishap inspired by the writing style of Erma Bombeck. A lifelong love of storytelling followed. Following a rewarding career in professional and technical communication, Judy devoted the second half of her career to teaching the art and craft of writing at the collegiate level. Now, the dream that began with a spilled bowl of soup has come full circle as she embraces a new chapter, writing and sharing stories that make readers laugh, reflect, grow in faith, and savor life's most unforgettable moments. More information can be found at: https://www.judytarbox.com/

Mary Jo Thayer, "The Glorious Pilgrimage of Margaret Henderson"

Mary Jo Thayer is an award-winning novelist, educator, and public speaker. She writes about the tough stuff of life, through a Theology of the Body lens. Connect with her on social media as @maryjothayerauthor or via her website: https://maryjothayer.com/

Corinna Turner, "A Very Jurassic Pilgrimage"

Corinna Turner is the Carnegie Medal-nominated author of the *Friends in High Places* series (Ignatius Press) and the *unSPARKed* and *I Am Margaret* series (UnSeen Books) among other titles.

For more in Kateri's world, try the first quick-read in the main *unSPARKed* series: *Please Don't Feed the Dinosaurs.* Or for a full-length pro-life adventure, pick up the prequel novel: *BREACH!* https://www.iammargaret.co.uk/

A.R.K. Watson, "The Promise"

Ever the contrarian, A.R.K. Watson began writing with both arms in braces as a broke college student. After converting to Catholicism from the Church of Christ, she drew upon the wisdom of Catholic literature to help her to make the transition from simply knowing her faith to feeling and living it. Her love of her faith and of art led her to start CatholicReads.com, a marketing service that connects Catholic authors to directly to readers, while writing sci-fi and mysteries herself. A world traveler, she has lived in Japan and South Korea. But above everything else she remains an absolute and unrepentant nerd.

Isabelle Wood, "Surrender"

Isabelle is the writing and editing specialist for Extraordinary Mission, a non-profit Catholic ministry. She is currently enrolled in a Christian, college-equivalent writing program, and it's her dream to write stories that shine the light of Jesus and the Catholic Church into the darkness of this world. You can find out more about her at https://www.imjwood.com/.

Catholic Writers Guild

ABOUT THE CATHOLIC WRITERS GUILD

The Catholic Writers Guild began in 2007 with about 30 members: writers who came together in an online forum to help each other with writing, marketing, and support. We incorporated as a 501(c)3 in 2009, taking the Guild from a chat group to an international organization dedicated to the rebirth of Catholic writing.

We've grown to over 500 members, including laypeople and religious, published and unpublished, nonfiction and fiction. Our only requirements are that members be true to Catholic teachings and that their work reflects that. While most of our members are writers or editors, we have publishers and illustrators as well. We're mostly USA-based, yet have members in Canada, Mexico, Trinidad, UK, Germany, Spain, Hong Kong, and Australia.

In August 2009, we ran the first Catholic Writers Conference Live in Somerset, NJ as well as the first Catholic Writers Conference Online. That first online conference took place through an online forum and chat room, and it included 47 presentations–more than the number of members just 2 years before! Now, a decade later, our online conference has moved to video conferencing and our live programs continue strong with conferences and retreats.

Learn more and join us at https://www.catholicwritersguild.org/.

www.ingramcontent.com/pod-product-compliance
Lightning Source LLC
Chambersburg PA
CBHW060212180626
46813CB00007B/2806